15 North

A NOVEL

Rev. Bob DeSagun, Ph.D.

Copyright © 2016 by Bob DeSagun
All rights reserved.
ISBN-13: 978-1539942139
ISBN-10: 1539942139

All Scripture quotations are taken from the Holy Bible, New International Version. Copyright © 1973, 1978, 1984, 2011 by Biblica, Inc.

Cover photograph by Bob DeSagun.

To my family and friends

"May the God of hope fill you with all joy
and peace as you trust in him, so that
you may overflow with hope by
the power of the Holy Spirit."

Romans 15:13 NIV

CONTENTS

CHAPTER 1
THE FUNERAL — 11

CHAPTER 2
JOHNNY B — 25

CHAPTER 3
THE BOOK — 39

CHAPTER 4
DARKNESS IN THE DESERT — 57

CHAPTER 5
NOMADS AND SOJOURNERS — 77

CHAPTER 6
MIRROR MIRROR ON THE WALL — 91

CHAPTER 7
ALL THIS AND JESUS TOO — 105

CHAPTER 8
THE BREAKDOWN — 121

CHAPTER 9
THE PK — 135

CHAPTER 10
JUST WANTING TO BE UNDERSTOOD — 149

CHAPTER 11
TIME WELL SPENT — 161

CHAPTER 12
PROBABILITY — 175

CHAPTER 13
THE GOVERNATOR   187

CHAPTER 14
INTO ANOTHER COUNTRY   201

CHAPTER 15
THE FUNERAL   211

What I mean, brothers and sisters, is that the time is short. From now on those who have wives should live as if they do not; those who mourn, as if they did not; those who are happy, as if they were not; those who buy something, as if it were not theirs to keep; those who use the things of the world, as if not engrossed in them.

                1 Corinthians 7:29-31

CHAPTER 1
The Funeral

Jack slowly and meticulously picked the lint from off of his jacket sleeve. He sat in silent apathy as he watched each lint flow into the breeze. Grief stricken, he had forgotten to run the lint roller over his black suit that morning after putting it on. It was a suit he typically wore to officiate weddings and conduct funerals. Today he was doing neither; instead, he was an attendee of the latter.

One of the most detachable emotions anyone can ever experience is loss. For Jack Hanson, his wife Karen meant the world to him. Jack and Karen met in high school, fell in love while in college, drove to Las Vegas one weekend and got married. Thirty years later, cancer took Karen's life.

It was a beautiful San Diego morning. There was a slight chill in the air as the sun shined brightly without a cloud in the sky. Nothing beats perfect year-round weather. But despite the perfect weather, a light jacket was suitable for today. The drive into El Camino Memorial Park was somber yet uncannily peaceful. The trees that lined the driveway entrance of the memorial park reminded Jack of the time he played a round of golf with his brother and Karen at the Torrey Pines North Course. Their game was cut short because Karen started to come down with a migraine. A close friend of Jack and Karen's generously donated the burial plot. It sat hillside along a narrow strip of road named Freedom Terrace just beneath the standing three-arched bell tower that was a distinctive landmark of the memorial park. As Jack looked across to the other side of the hill, he could see the company building where Karen used to work. Fond memories filled his mind as he reminisced about the times he would pick Karen up for lunch. Jack and Karen had lunch together every day. The only time they wouldn't have lunch together was when Jack either had a meeting or was out of town. They enjoyed one another's company, and lunch was a great break in their day for them to connect before heading back to work. After they ate lunch, they would take time to pray for one another, their daughter Hannah, their families, their church, and any other pressing issues at the time. Jack and Karen believed that a couple that prays together stays together. It was their habit to pray together every day. They prayed morning, noon, and night. Well at least they prayed most every night. If they didn't, it was Jacks fault. He would always fall asleep early while Karen stayed up late.

Black attire and sunglasses appeared to be the typical dress for that day. Then again, it was a funeral. The guests gathered to console the grieving and pay their respects to the deceased. Typically Jack would be the presiding minister. He had officiated many funerals throughout his career as a pastor. This time it was different, not because he was retired, but because the deceased was his beloved wife Karen. Struggling to decide whether or not he could preside over the ceremony himself, he eventually realized it was out of the question. Jack officiated his dad's funeral and remembered the difficulty of keeping his composure throughout the ceremony. There was no way he could have held it together through this one, especially because it was his dear wife Karen who was being laid to rest. Jack was always an ugly crier. It was impossible to make out anything he said while he was crying. On occasion, Jack would preach a sermon that eventually brought him to tears. Congregation members didn't quite know how to respond because no one could make clear a word he was trying to say. His ugly cry resembled the sound of one of those barking sea lions on the docks of San Francisco's Pier 39.

The minister who presided over Karen's funeral did an absolutely beautiful job. He conducted it exactly the way Jack would have had done it. It was as if he took a page right out of Jack's book. Terry was a loyal and close friend of Jack and Karen. He was Jack's associate pastor who help start the church and then later took over as the senior pastor after Jack retired. Jack and Terry previously served together at another church while working youth ministry together for over 10 years. So they shared many fond memories together. During the ceremony, Terry shared funny stories of when he, his wife Abby, along with Jack and Karen would drive over thirty high school students from San Diego to Portland for youth camp. Every summer they would pack the students into four passenger vans and make the road trip up the western coast. Terry shared how on one particular trip his wife and Karen were terrified of deer while camping at Mt. Shasta. The two ladies quickly ran from the restroom scared out of their wits as if they had saw a ghost, only to realize they were running from the sight of a deer. Laughing hysterically, one of the students remarked, "I can't believe you're afraid of Bambi." Karen responded back by saying, "Have you ever seen the show 'Animals Gone Wild'?" Everyone laughed as Terry shared the humorous stories about Karen that put a brief smile on Jack's face as he vividly remembered those early days of ministry together with her. Those were the days when they were young, new to ministry and having the time of their lives with not a care in the world and cancer free. It was a beautiful ceremony filled with laughter and tears. Terry did a wonderful job of honoring and celebrating the life of Karen.

After the laughter died down, Jack sat there completely empty and numb. He didn't know what to say. He didn't know what to think. He didn't know what to feel. He was completely void inside as if the greatest part of him was stolen away. He never imagined that he would have found himself in this predicament. With his cholesterol and they way he ate, Jack thought for sure he was going to die first from a heart attack. He never imagined that Karen would go before him. He never thought that there would ever be a moment where he would have to live a life without her. Jack began to feel the hurt as the numbness began to fade. A glassy teardrop began to stream down his cheek behind his sunglasses. The hurt ran deep. Never before had Jack experience a pain so intense and so indescribable. It was probably the first time Jack had ever felt anything for a couple of days now. All he knew was that his heart broke. He tried to pull himself together inside, but it only got worse. The stronger he tried to be, the stronger the hurt intensified, and the tears really began to flow. Hannah put her arm around him as she sat next to Jack. She leaned over and whispered in his ear, "Dad, remember your favorite Scripture verse that you use to say to yourself every time I gave you a heartache when I was growing up? Say that to yourself now." Mustering up the strength, Jack was able to barely squeeze out a grin from Hannah's suggestion. With all the strength and courage that he had left, he closed his eyes and imagined Jesus placing His hand on Jack's shoulder and saying those words from John 14:1-4 to him:

> *Do not let your hearts be troubled. You believe in God; believe also in me. My Father's house has many rooms; if that were not so, would I have told you that I am going there to prepared a place for*

you? And if I go and prepare a place for you, I will come back and take you to be with me that you may be where I am. You know the way to the place where I am going.

The words of this passage have always brought great relief and comfort to Jack. Whenever life got tough, Jack would imagine Jesus reminding him of that precious promise. It was his favorite passage of Scripture. It personally put everything in proper perspective for him. It was a wonderful reminder not to worry about the things in this life because a more beautiful and glorious life awaits us. This passage reminded Jack that he was loved. It reminded him that he was made for a beautiful place and a wonderful person. That place was heaven and that person was Jesus his Lord and Savior. The consolation now was that Karen was there ready and waiting for him on the other side.

All of Jack and Karen's family were present at the funeral that morning. A majority of Karen's family was from San Diego. Jack had two brothers drive down from San Jose, and the rest of his family came from Las Vegas. Despite the occasion, Jack was delighted to see all of his family together in one place. Their annual Thanksgiving family reunion was the only other time they were together. Jack appreciated their show of love and support as they paid their respects and condolences to him and his family. Jack was very close with his family. Aside from the annual family reunion, the family would either visit Jack in San Diego or Jack would fly up to San Jose to spend time with his two brothers. Jack's two brothers from San Jose were very concerned for him. They knew how much he loved Karen. They both knew that life without her was going to be difficult for him. But all of Jack's family made sure that he could depend on them for anything during this time of grief.

Everyone headed back to Jack's home for the reception after the ceremony. Jack didn't want to leave. He did not want to leave Karen. He stayed for at least another hour after the last person left the gravesite. Concerned for her dad, Hannah stayed by his side until he was ready to go. He was never ready. He never will be.

Jack was so attached to Karen that they were inseparable. Karen and Hannah were the primary reasons he had resigned his commission in the Marine Corps after his initial four-year commitment. Jack was constantly on deployment cycles that kept him away from his family. It killed him to be separated from them.

While in ministry, Jack would travel out of town for meetings and conferences. Although he loved and enjoyed attending them, he couldn't stand being away from Karen for a single day. On days when they couldn't have lunch together, Jack would miss her so much as if though he had been gone for weeks. He couldn't stand being away from her for more than a couple of hours. He would call her in the middle of the day just to hear her voice and tell her how much he loves her. Jack could not live without Karen.

But now he didn't have a choice. Jack had made it a practice never to get so attached to things. Attachment can lend itself to a form of enslavement. Jack remembered the Bible passage that reminds us not to store up treasures on earth where moth and vermin destroy and thieves break in and steal but rather in heaven, for where your treasure is, there your heart will be also. He remembered taking his church on a mission trip to Ensenada, Mexico where they brought food, clothes and toys to families of an outlying village in the mountains of Baja California. He had just bought his dream car - a brand new Honda Element. Durango was a remote off-road town near the city of Ensenada. So whenever Jack's church would visit there on a mission trip, every inch of their cars would eventually be covered in dirt by the end of the day. Jack noticed some kids from the town drawing on his dirt-covered Honda Element with their fingers that day. The fine dirt would scratch into the paint of the car. Jack's first thought was, "Oh no! My new car!" It took a moment, but Jack's realized the priceless moment of seeing the joy in the faces of the kids as they drew wonderful images on the surface of his car. For Jack, it was a lesson in detaching from the things of this world that we can't bring over to the next. Jack was reminded of the passage in 1 Corinthians 7:29-31:

> *What I mean, brothers and sisters, is that the time is short. From now on those who have wives should live as if they do not; those who mourn, as if they did not; those who are happy, as if they were not; those who buy something, as if it were not theirs to keep; those who use the things of the world, as if not engrossed in them.*

Jack knew that the key to living was not to get attached to the things of this life. We should not let the temporal things take the place of the eternal things. We should not let holding on to the earthly things keep us from continually reaching for the heavenly things.[1] We shouldn't get so bound up with the material things here on earth that have a tendency to weigh us down and keep us from the things that really matter. It was a matter of traveling light in this life.

    Jack and Karen knew how to travel light in life. They lived a minimalist kind of lifestyle. At one point in their marriage, after buying their first home, they realized all the things they had accumulated over the years. Jack learned early during his single-life in the military how to live off of only what he could fit in his sea bag, which is basically an oversized military duffle bag. He constantly reminded Karen how he loves traveling with only a carry-on size bag and a backpack. In those two bags he could carry everything he essentially needed to survive. With this mentality, they both decided that they needed to start downsizing. Karen called it "minimalizing." They worked through each room of their home either to get rid of or donate things that were nonessential to their life. Jack remembered how Karen taught him how to determine what things to keep and what things to get rid of. It was a practice Karen learned through watching a gal on YouTube who specialized in organizing and decluttering spaces. As they tackled each room of the house,

Karen instructed Jack to physically touch and hold each item. If the item didn't give him some kind of emotional connection or a sense of happiness, then it was something to let go and get rid of. Periodically they would go throughout the house and get rid of nonessential things. Jack would go through the practice of physically touching and holding things to see if it either provided him with some kind of emotional connection or gave him some sense of happiness. If it didn't, then it would either go in the trash or get donated to Goodwill. Karen always said that Jack was the "girl" in the relationship. He was the one who always like to go shopping. He would buy plenty of clothes and shoes. So it wasn't easy for Jack to go through all of his clothes and get rid of over half of his wardrobe. He eventually did and learned to live without having so much. But having to let Karen go was never a thought. Every time he touched or held her, Jack would always experience an emotional connection that would make him happy. If only he could touch and hold her one last time.

Who do you say I am?

Matthew 16:15

CHAPTER 2
Johnny B

Jack loved the way Karen smelled. Karen never used perfume, but she had a scent that Jack loved. As her clothes hung in their bedroom closet, Jack could still smell her scent. On occasion, he would sniff her deodorant that was left in the medicine cabinet or her shampoo that was left in the shower. Karen's scent had a calming effect on him. Jack would have Karen accompany him to his annual physical check-ups where he would have Karen stand next to him so that he could smell her hair as the doctor took his blood pressure. Jack believed that smelling Karen's hair had a calming effect on him that would lower his blood pressure.

Jack and Karen's home of over 20 years was filled with wonderful memories of her. Pictures of Karen hung on the walls, sat on the shelves in the living room and on the nightstands in their bedroom. Her college diplomas hung on the wall in their home office. The jewelry she wore every day laid in a ceramic dish that sat on the nightstand next to her side of the bed. Practically everything in the house served as a reminder of Karen and how much Jack missed her. With Karen gone, it was difficult for Jack to live in the home they had made for themselves; a home that was now filled with remnants of her. How was he supposed to move on with his life when the home he lived in was a huge reminder of her?

    Jack had to get away. He always loved the idea of travel, but he didn't care for flying. It wasn't because he was scared to fly; he just didn't care for being cooped up on an airplane. Jack could never sleep on a plane. He could never get comfortable enough to fall asleep during flights. Jack found it impossible to sleep unless he was lying down. Jack could sleep in the middle of Times Square on New Year's Eve minutes before the ball dropped as long as he was lying down. But one thing Jack loved was airports. He enjoyed long layovers where he could either catch up on some reading, grab a bite to eat, have some coffee, or just people watch. He loved the airport because he felt a sense of self-sustainability at them when he traveled. All that Jack needed in life was his carry-on bag with a couple of changes of clean clothes and his toothbrush, a backpack with his laptop computer, his cellphone in his pocket, and Karen by his side. If his house were to burn down while he and Karen were traveling, he wouldn't miss anything. The fire could take it all, and it would not matter to him. Sadly, this time around, Jack would be traveling without Karen by his side.

When Jack needed some time alone to himself to think, he would get into this car and just go on a drive. Jack was not much of a music person, so he never turned the radio on when he drove. He enjoyed the silence, for it allowed him to hear himself think and pray on occasion. At times, he would just drive and purposefully get himself lost in order to discover some part of the city of San Diego that he had never seen before. Sometimes he would just get out of the house and just drive. And that's what he needed to do. He just needed to get away.

Jack decided to plan an indefinite road trip. He was enamored by a young couple on YouTube who lived and traveled out of their vintage Volkswagen camper van. The gal was a web-designer who worked anywhere she could find a Wi-Fi connection, and her boyfriend took care of the maintenance of the van and cooked the meals. They were free-spirited modern day gypsies who traveled the United States living out of their camper van while documenting their journeys and experiences on YouTube. On several occasions, Jack tried to convince Karen to do that with him when they retired. Karen thought the idea was intriguing, but she just didn't care to do it indefinitely. So Jack figured if he was going to do it, now was the best time.

Jack did some online research to find an RV that would suit him best. He found someone on Craigslist trying to sell a 20 foot 1989 Chevy Fleetwood Jamboree. Jack sent the seller an e-mail requesting to meet up so that he could check out the vehicle. Within a matter of minutes, the seller replied back and was available to meet with Jack that day.

The seller lived out in Ramona, which was approximately 40 minutes northeast of San Diego. The drive up was through rolling hills covered with boulders that peaked through the green small trees and brush. The seller lived right off of Highway 67 on Peace Valley Lane. The turnoff was sharp and sloped down an underdeveloped and barely paved driveway.

Jack parked out front and made his way up the cobblestone walkway that lead to the house. As he stepped up unto the creaky front porch, he approached the dusty screen door, which made it difficult to see inside the house. As he knocked on the doorframe, an older outdoorsy-type looking man greeted him at the door. He extended his hand saying, "Jack I assume? I'm Brad. Glad you were able to come and check out Johnny B."

Extending out his hand, Jack replied back, "Glad to meet you too Brad, but who's Johnny B?"

With a huge grin, Brad replied, "Johnny B is what I named my RV."

"Interesting," Jack said assumedly. "I heard of people naming their boats but never RVs."

"That's funny you mentioned that," said Brad, "I also have a boat, but I never named it."

Brad led Jack to the side of the house where he stored Johnny B. Turning the corner of the house, Jack noticed that Brad also had a 36 foot fishing boat, an old 1960 Ford pick up truck, a 2000 Harley Davidson Road King Classic, a 1999 Honda Fourtrax 300 quad, and a Vespa scooter.

"Nice collection!" Jack commented as his eyes widened in excitement.

"I take the boat out twice a month down in Baja for some tuna fishing, I'm restoring the pick-up as a hobby, the Harley is my everyday vehicle as well as my weekend recreational ride, the quad is essential to getting out on the off roads and having to live out here in the boondocks, and the Vespa is my wife's. I wouldn't be caught dead on that thing."

Brad unlocked the RV, swung open the door and motioned a welcoming hand gesture for Jack to climb in. As Jack stepped up into the RV, he could see the kitchenette immediately to the left side that was equipped with a propane gas stove and a small refrigerator beneath the countertops. A bench-style dinette table was situated on the right side next to the window. The toilet, shower and vanity sink were all enclosed in a tiny closet-sized room to the far back right. And to the far back left of the cabin was a full-size mattress bed. There appeared to initially be an overhead bed above the driver and passenger cabin, but Brad explained to Jack that he had it converted into some extra overhead cabinet space. The interior walls were lined with old wood-laminate sidings, and the carpet was in pretty bad shape. It was old, but it was just what Jack was looking for.

"Does everything work?" asked Jack.

"For the most part," chuckled Brad.

"Any special meaning behind why you named it Johnny B?"

Brad explained to Jack that when he and his wife Jen bought it new back in 1989, they had plans to travel around the country with the purpose of engaging random strangers in spiritual conversations. They wanted to see where people were spiritually and how much they really knew about Jesus Christ. When opportunity presented itself, he and Jen would share the gospel message with anyone who would listen. They drove all over the U.S. engaging people in dialog and sharing Jesus whenever and wherever they could. They were like John the Baptist from the Bible; hence the name "Johnny B." Brad even had the license plate personalized with JOHNNYB.

Out of the blue, Brad boldly and unashamedly asked Jack, "What do you know about Jesus?"

"Well, to tell you the truth," Jack started, "I'm a retired pastor."

"I didn't ask you what you use to do for a living," Brad quirked, "I asked you what you know about Jesus. Who is He to you?"

Jack should have known better than to answer the way he did. Immediately he was reminded of a sermon he had preached from a passage out of the Book of Matthew 16:15 where Jesus asked His disciples who do people say that He is? The disciples replied that some say He is John the Baptist, while others say He is Elijah, Jeremiah or one of the other prophets. But then Jesus asked them, "But who do you say I am?" That is the most important question in the whole wide world that anybody could ever answer. It's not about what other people say who Jesus is; it's about whom you say Jesus is. What is your response to who Jesus is to you? Was he just an historical Jewish rabbi from the first century? Was he just a good teacher? Maybe he is just a fictitious character from an ancient book known throughout the world as the Holy Bible. Who is Jesus to you? From the Bible in Matthew 16:16, the disciple Peter responded that Jesus was the Messiah, the Son of the Living God. It's a question that you can't answer from your head; it has to come from your heart. It has to come from the very fiber of your soul that has an undeniable and indescribable hunger or thirst that longs to be quenched. Jesus' question, "Who do you say that I am?" is the most profound question that anybody could ever ask you, and your response to that question is the most pivotal answer that you can ever give.[2]

And that is the question that Brad just asked Jack.

Jack looked at Brad and replied, "Where do I even start?"

"Now that was more of the kind of response I was looking for," said Brad.

For Jack, Jesus meant everything to him. His faith in Christ was the single most important thing to him in the whole wide world. He knew that Jesus the Son of the Living God was the very reason and purpose for his life. Jack gained his identity through his relationship with Christ. In knowing Christ, it helped Jack know the truth of who he was and why he was put on this earth to live. The magnitude of what Jesus meant to Jack was both incomprehensible and indescribable. To know Jesus as the Messiah is not only a great honor but also a wonderful privilege. The Messiah is a Jewish title that refers to an expected future deliverer sent by God who would restore the nation of Israel, but the New Testament Scriptures reveal the Messiah to be so much more. He would be the Son of God, the Savior of all of the world's people. He would save everyone from the terrible effects of their sins. Jesus accomplished this through His obedient and willful sacrifice when He was crucified on the cross for the forgiveness of sin and life everlasting to those who would believe in Him. For Jack, Jesus was a game changer who positively affects every single aspect of his life. Jack came to know Jesus when he served as an officer in the Marine Corps. He was deployed to Okinawa, Japan for six months away from Karen and his infant daughter Hannah. While in Okinawa, he began attending chapel services on the Marine base because he thought it was a good way to pass the time away while staying out of trouble. After his deployment, and upon returning home to Hawaii, he and Karen began attending a small Bible-based church in Kailua, Hawaii. Hearing the gospel message of Jesus Christ for the first time was like a light that pierced through the darkness and hardness of his heart. Jack had some knowledge about religious things like sin, the cross, Jesus, the Bible, and church. It was not until he began to faithfully attend this small church and listen to the pastor preach did he finally begin to piecemeal it all together. The grace-filled message of the gospel of "who Jesus is" and "what Jesus did" all came together for Jack which led him to a greater and fuller understanding of it all. During that time, Jack was able to personally answer for himself who Jesus was to him. For Jack, Jesus was his God, his Lord, and his Savior. Since then, Jack learned that Jesus was also his Healer, his Redeemer, his Sanctifier, his Provider, his victory, his peace, his joy, his purpose, his meaning, his fulfillment, his life, his source, his Rock, his protection, his fortress, his refuge, his Truth, and eventually Jesus will be his Coming King. Jesus was everything to Jack.

Brad knew that he didn't need to press Jack any further with his answer. It was clear that Jack had a strong personal relationship with Christ.

"So what do you think about Johnny B?" asked Brad.

"Looks a like it needs a little work. Craigslist says you're asking for $6,500. Would you take $5,000?"

Brad countered by saying, "How about we meet half-way at $5,750?"

Jack paused for a moment to think about the offer. Then Brad asked, "Just out of curiosity, how many miles do you have on that Honda Element of yours parked outside?"

"Around 140,000. Why?"

Brad asked, "Did you know Honda no longer makes those?"

"Yup" said Jack. "I bought this one brand new when it first came out in 2003. It's a pretty versatile kind of utility vehicle."

"I know," said Brad. "Would you consider an even trade?"

"My Element for the RV?" Jack asked surprised.

Brad nodded his head.

Jack thought for a second how attached he was to his Honda Element. He remembered a conversation he had a while ago with a congregation member regarding what his "dream car" would be. She asked Jack if he could have any car in the world, what car would he choose? He told her it would be the Honda Element that he already owned. Jack remembered how dumbfounded she was by his answer. He could have said a Ferrari or Lamborghini, but Jack was insistent on the Honda Element. He loved the shape and versatility of the vehicle.

After thinking it over, Jack said, "You have yourself a deal!"

They shook hands on the deal. They filled out and exchanged vehicle titles. After submitting the appropriate forms to the local DMV, Jack was now the proud owner of a 1989 Chevy Fleetwood Jamboree named "Johnny B."

All Scripture is God-breath...

2 Timothy 3:16

CHAPTER 3
The Book

After some deep cleaning and a couple of maintenance trips to the local RV service center, Johnny B was ready for the open road. Jack did some quick planning to map out his drive. He decided on a route up Interstate 15 northbound. That route from San Diego would take him through states that he had never visited before like the "Big Sky Country" state of Montana.

Jack packed light. All he took with him were mere essentials. Filled with mixed emotions, he hugged and kissed Hannah and his grandson Jimmy and told them how much he loved them both. With tears in his eyes, Jack handed over the keys to the home that they had all shared as a family. Feeling both sad and excited, Jack got into Johnny B ready to face the road ahead. With one last look, he smiled at Hannah and Jimmy as he drove off into his destiny.

Jack always enjoyed long drives and road trips. He attributes his love for the road to his dad. When he was a kid, his dad would pile all the kids into the family station wagon just to go on a drive. Jack made several road trips across the country. A few of those trips were with his family during his early teenage years and then a couple of times when he was in training during his time in the Marine Corps. But this time he would take a different route. He was headed northbound on Interstate 15 as far as it would take him. Jack had no agenda; he simply wanted to just get away. For him, it was a way of processing his grief and loss. It was also a way to start anew. The road trip would allow him an opportunity to clear his head and start a new chapter in his life.

The first few hours of the drive up Interstate 15 from San Diego was quite exciting for Jack. The thought of a new horizon and seeing and experiencing new sites made Jack feel like he was on an adventure. The enthusiasm to fulfill a long time dream to live off of the open road was in front of him. He looked forward to a carefree life filled with new journeys into uncharted territory. It was also the first time he had ever drove an RV. But it didn't take long for his thoughts to wander back to Karen. His heart once again battled against a heaviness that sucked his soul dry. It was a heaviness of a loss he could have never imaged. He missed her so much that it hurt. The feelings of excitement began to deteriorate back into grief. Jack started to remember all the times when he and Karen would drive this route to Las Vegas for Jack's yearly Thanksgiving family reunions. Most of his family lived in Las Vegas. But those memories weren't the ones that triggered his sadness. It was remembering their first drive to Las Vegas where he and Karen went to get married. Jack and Karen met when they were in high school. Both of their dads were stationed overseas on a military base where Jack and Karen attended high school. After high school, they went their separate ways but were coincidentally reacquainted in college when a mutual friend set them up on a blind date. The moment Jack laid eyes on her he instantly fell in love. Karen dropped out of college at San Diego State University to help financially support Jack through his last year at the University of San Diego. That year, they decided to drive up to Las Vegas and get married. The rest was history. Jack always loved telling that story, but Karen would always have to correct him regarding some of the details. His love for her was so deep that his loss became so weighty upon his fragile and broken heart.

Jack looked down at the dashboard and noticed that his gas needle was getting near the "E" mark. He decided to take the next exit off of Lenwood Road. He pulled into the TA Travel Center in Barstow. Johnny B's gas mileage was not as impressive as his old Honda Element.

After filling up his tank, Jack decided to grab a bite to eat inside. Upon entering through the glass doors, he noticed a chrome metal frame sign at the entrance for Truckstop Ministry, Inc. It appeared to be a transdenominational ministry that reached out to truck drivers with the gospel of Jesus Christ. According to the sign, they met every Sunday at 9:00am in the restaurant's banquet room. It served as church for truck drivers who were on the road and away from home. As Jack entered, he saw the Country Pride restaurant to the left, which was very similar to a Denny's restaurant. While Jack stood at the entrance waiting to be seated, he noticed a table displaying packages of fresh fudge for sale. A young gal wearing an apron came up to Jack and directed him to a nearby booth and handed him a menu.

"Welcome to Country Pride. I'll be your server. Can I get you something to drink while you look over the menu?" asked the waitress.

"A glass of water and a cup of coffee would be fine," replied Jack. "And what's your name?" Jack asked. Jack always made it a point to find out and address his servers by their name.

"Melissa," she replied.

"Thank you Melissa."

"I'll grab your drinks. Let me know if you have any questions about the menu," Melissa said as she turned towards the kitchen area.

Melissa returned with Jack's water and coffee. "Have you decided what you want?"

"I'll have the pot roast dinner please," said Jack.

"I'll have the right up for you," Melissa said as she grabbed Jack's menu and then turned again towards the kitchen to place the order.

When she returned with his order, Jack inquired about the Truckstop Ministry that met at the restaurant. He loved engaging complete strangers in any form of conversation. There was one time when he and Karen were having dinner at the bar counter at a restaurant at San Diego's Seaport Village when a young couple came in and sat next to them. After they had ordered their drinks, the bartender asked to see their IDs, and immediately Jack noticed their Wisconsin driver licenses. Jack leaned over towards the couple to let them know that he noticed that they were from out of town. Jack asked what brought them to San Diego. It happened that the guy was in town for a work conference and his wife just tagged along as a make-up honeymoon trip that they weren't able to take after their wedding. Jack congratulated them on their recent marriage. They asked Jack where were some good places to eat downtown, and Jack told them about San Diego's Gaslamp District. But Jack insisted that, while they were in San Diego, they needed to find the nearest Roberto's Taco Shop and try their rolled tacos with guacamole and cheese. He also emphasized to make sure they eat it with the homemade hot sauce. There's nothing like it. Jack was a foodie. He was one who always enjoyed making recommendations for places to eat at.

"Well it's a bunch of folks, mainly guys, truckers, that get together here every Sunday and talk about the Bible," Melissa explained. "I'll be over there a couple of booths down from you, so just wave to me if you need anything."

"Thank you, " replied Jack.

Melissa grabbed a book she had behind the counter and sat a couple of booths down from Jack. She opened the book to where she had left off and continued reading.

Jack was the only person in the restaurant. After a while, Melissa got up and grabbed a water pitcher and came over to refill Jack's water cup. "How's everything?" she asked.

"Everything's wonderful," Jack replied. Do you mind if I ask what you're reading?

"No, not at all," Melissa replied. It's called *Looking For Alaska*.

"What's it about?" asked Jack.

"It's basically about this guy named Miles, and he decides to attend a boarding school and meets and falls in love with this girl named Alaska who is a bit…," Melissa paused to think of the right word to describe the character, "…peculiar."

"Peculiar," said Jack as he nodded his head a little befuddled. "Is that good or bad?"

"I guess neither," replied Melissa.

"Do you like the book so far?"

"Yeah, I'm enjoying it."

"Do you read a lot?" Jack asked.

"I do. I really enjoy reading. How about you?"

"Oh yeah, I really enjoy reading. I used to not like to read since back when I was in college. I used to make fun of people who liked 'recreational reading.' I considered that an oxymoron. But then later in my life I started to really catch on to it."

"Since then, I could imagine you've probably read a lot of books huh?" Melissa asked.

"Are you implying that I'm old?" asked Jack with a grin.

"Oh, no. I just meant…" she could barely finish her sentence before Jack cut her off.

"I'm just joking with you. I have read quite a few books. I have a home office where me and a friend built a small library to house all of the books I own." Jack pulled out his phone and showed her a picture of the library he and his friend built in his home office.

"Wow! That looks pretty cool," Melissa said as she checked out the picture. "Do you happen to remember the very first book you read that 'did you in'?" Melisa asked.

"I sure do. It was the Bible," Jack replied.

"Wow," responded Melissa. "That's a pretty big book."

"Yeah, but it's quite an amazing read."

"I don't mean to sound ignorant," said Melissa, "But is there some proper way that you need to read it? I mean like, where do you even start? Isn't it like some 'rule book' of what you shouldn't do if you're religious or something? Like doesn't it tell you stuff like not to smoke, cheat, lie or steal?"

Jack couldn't help but giggle a little bit. "It's actually far from that Melissa. From what you've told me, it's a lot like the book you're reading right now."

"In what way?" asked Melissa.

"It's a love story," replied Jack

"Really? I've never heard anyone say that before about the Bible? How is that?" asked Melissa.

"Well, to get right to it, the Bible is God's true story of how much He loves everyone, and He demonstrates that love my an amazing act of sacrifice. The story is filled with drama, plots, twists, turns, and surprises like no other. I would highly recommend reading it. I think you'd be amazed by what you'll discover"

"Sounds intriguing," replied Melissa.

"What would you say if I told you that God has something to say to you through the words of the Bible that could have a major impact on your life?" enticed Jack.

"Then I'd definitely be interested," said Melissa.

"Care to sit down and chat more about it? Or are you not allowed to do that with customers?" Jack asked.

"I should be fine. It's pretty late, and were definitely not busy as you can see," Melissa said as she motioned her head revealing an empty restaurant.

Slowly taking a seat, Melissa sat directly across from Jack. He began to explain to her how the Bible is unlike any other book in history. It's a book filled with words that have the potential to reach deep into the human soul, expose us for who we really are, transform our hearts, renew our minds, and lead us into a deep personal and meaningful relationship like no other. It's a book that invites people into a personal relationship with a loving and compassionate God. It's a dynamic book that's inspiring, invigorating, liberating, magnetic, alive, and resonates with divine power and authority with an undeniable truth that is infallible, inerrant, and eternal. Jack explained how the Bible is a product of three different continents, written originally in three different languages now translated in over 2,400 languages with an amazing array of literary styles and genres that include laws, historical events, incredible true-life stories, poems, prayers, sermons, parables, and letters that were all written within a time span of over 1,500 years by 40 different authors who personalities were as diverse as the cultures that produced them, yet cohesively speaks one divinely inspired and unified message.

"What message is that?" Melissa asked.

"That God loves you," replied Jack. "You can't imagine how much God loves you." Jack shared the message of the gospel of Jesus Christ with her. He explained how God demonstrated His love for the entire human race by sending His Son Jesus to die on the cross for the forgiveness of everyone's sin, and that whoever would believe in Him and put their faith in Him would have eternal life. This is a gift from God that can neither be bought nor earned. Jack continued to explain how this was the central message of the Bible, and that everything that you read in the Bible uniquely ties back to this one central message of how God loves you.

Melissa replied surprisingly, "I have never heard that message before."

Jack explained how he had been reading the Bible for over 25 years; and every year he reads it, he is convinced that no other book can compare to it, stand alongside it, nor contend against it, for it contains the very breath of God. It literally is the "Word of God." Pausing for a moment, Jack took a couple of bites of his pot roast.

Melissa was surprised by Jack's passion and knowledge of the Bible. "Are you some kind of priest or something?" she asked.

"I'm a retired pastor," Jack replied nonchalantly as he took a few more bites of his meal. "The more you read and study it, the more you'll discover the wonderful things that God desires to say to you personally."

Jack shared how his wife Karen was very talkative when she was a kid. Karen would talk so much that she constantly got into trouble with her teachers for talking in class. In elementary school, the children would sit together around tables in small groups. Karen loved to talk to her classmate, so her teacher had to constantly move her to another table in hopes that she would stop talking and disrupting class. Karen, being the social butterfly that she was, quickly assimilated with her classmates at her new table and continued to talk and socialize with them. As a last resort, Karen's teacher thought, "If I move her to a place right in front of my desk all by herself, then that will get her to stop talking." So her teacher moved her directly in front of her desk. That didn't help because now Karen started talking and socializing with her teacher. Having run out of options, the teacher decided to put Karen at a desk in the font corner of the classroom facing the wall. The only problem with that was there was a full-length mirror in the corner. Karen faced the mirror, smiled, made faces at herself and pretended to talk as if she was talking to someone in the mirror. Karen always had something to say.

"Just like my wife Karen, God always has something to say to us. He is constantly speaking to us," explained Jack. "And He has incredibly wonderful things to say to us. The question is are we listening?"

Jack told Melissa what former President Woodrow Wilson had to say about the Bible. He said, "A man has found himself when he as found his relation to the rest of the universe, and here is a book in which those relationships are set forth." The Bible is God's words to us. If you want to hear from God, then look no further but to the words of the Bible. God speaks to us through our circumstances and predicaments as well as through other people, but what He says should always be confirmed by what is revealed to us in the Bible. Jack also explained how God will oftentimes speak to us through our thoughts and consciences too; so don't expect an audible voice though nothing is impossible with God. God is constantly communicating to us, constantly speaking to us through various forms, and the Bible is the most distinctive means by which we can clearly hear and discern His voice.[3]

"So what you're telling me is that God has something to say to me, and I'll find it in the Bible?" asked Melissa as if it was something hard to believe. To her, the message seemed too simple. She thought hearing from God was going to be more complex.

"Like I said, God is constantly speaking to us, and the Bible is a great place to start if we really want to hear what He is saying," Jack reassured her. "Check out the group that meets here every Sunday or find a church nearby that teaches from the Bible. I'm certain either one of those groups will help you as you read the Bible for yourself."

"Thanks Jack. I mean Pastor Jack," she said with a smile. "I most certainly will do that."

Jack finished up his pot roast dinner, paid his bill, and left Melissa with a generous tip.

Jack was ready to turn in for the night. It had been a very long day for him. But despite being tired, jack was excited about his first night sleeping in Johnny B. The sounds of the trucks, cars, and travelers coming in and out of the travel center could be heard throughout the evening as Jack left the windows of the RV slightly open that evening. In his excitement, he was having trouble trying to get to sleep. Suddenly a thought came across his mind as he stared up at the ceiling of his RV. It was a thought that prompted him to get up, grab his Bible from out of his backpack, and head back inside the restaurant. He walked up to Melissa and handed her the Bible saying, "I want you to have this."

Melissa took it into her hands as if it were fragile. It looked so old and ancient. The leather cover was soft, worn, and frayed at the edges. The imprint of the title "Holy Bible" was barely readable on the spine. As Melissa flipped through the pages, she noticed how much of it was underlined, circled, and highlighted. She also saw handwritten notes in the margins. Immediately she thought that this was a very personal item, and now it was a personal gift to her.

"Is this yours?" Melissa asked.

"Yes, and now it's yours," said Jack. "I really want you to have it."

"I couldn't possibly..." Melissa said before Jack interrupted her.

"Please accept it," Jack almost pleaded.

"I don't know what to say," responded Melissa as she clutched it and brought it into her chest as a gesture of gratitude.

"Just say you'll read it."

"I will definitely read it. Thank you."

With that, Jack headed back to his RV and was able to fall right to sleep.

You, LORD, are my lamp; the LORD turns my darkness into light.

2 Samuel 22:29

CHAPTER 4
Darkness In The Desert

Jack slept like a baby that evening. He's not one to sleep in. He is an early riser and enjoys getting ready to start the day. He grabbed a coffee from the Country Pride restaurant to go but didn't see Melissa there that morning. Jack was ready to take Johnny B back on the open road, so he immediately headed towards the interstate. Relaxed in his seat and with both hands on the steering wheel, Jack kept a steady course northward. He started thinking about his conversation with Melissa last night. Through years of reading and studying the Bible, Jack developed a keen sense of when God was speaking to him. He hopes that Melissa will do the same.

After a couple of hours driving up the interstate through the desert, Jack approached the California/Nevada state line. There were a couple of casinos and an outlet mall out in the middle of nowhere. Jack turned off onto the exit near Whiskey Pete's Casino. As he pulled over, he immediately began to reminisce about his family trips back when he was a kid. Leaning forward on his steering wheel, Jack sat for a moment. A little lost in his thoughts, he shook his head and smiled as the fond memories of him and his siblings began to flood into his mind. Feeling a little stiff from the drive, he thought a little walk and fresh air would do him some good.

Jack remembered Whiskey Pete's Casino back when he and his family would make a pit stop here on their way to Las Vegas. The only thing was that his dad would lose all his money at Whisky Pete's and then they would drive back home never making it to Las Vegas. Back when Jack was a kid, Whiskey Pete's Casino was the only thing that sat on the state line. Now the state line has been built up with other casinos and establishments. Because there wasn't much to do here back when Jack was a kid, he and his siblings would play cowboys and Indians out in the middle of the desert.

After a brief stretch and a short walk around the area, Jack got back into Johnny B and kicked his feet up on the dashboard. He ended up falling asleep in the driver's seat reminiscing about when he was a kid and playing out in the desert. When he woke up, he was surprised to see that the sun had already set. He sat in bewilderment trying to figure out how long he had fallen asleep. He was thrown aback by that fact that he had slept so long after having woken up late that morning. He didn't feel tired when he arrived at the state line. Something must have come over him. He had lost most of the day. Darkness had crept upon him so quickly and unexpectedly. He immediately decided to get back on the interstate. Jack arrived in Las Vegas within an hour.

    The Las Vegas city lights set the horizon aglow as Jack neared. The radiant Sky Beam from the Luxor Hotel was a very distinctive and iconic sight. It is said that it is one of only a couple of manmade objects that can actually be seen from outer space. Taking in the sights as he approached the city, a sudden and familiar eerie sensation came over him. It was a feeling that was uncannily comforting and yet unnerving at the same time. It was a sensation that would come upon him during times of vulnerability. Having lost Karen recently, he was in the most vulnerable state of his life. This feeling pulled on him and rendered him without control. He immediately recognized the feeling as it became increasingly familiar. It was a demon that had been buried for a long time and now has suddenly awaken like a bear coming out of hibernation.

Jack was heavily into gambling before making a commitment to become a Christian. Growing up, Jack's family vacations consisted of places with casinos like Las Vegas and Atlantic City. Jack remembers frequenting the arcades as a kid on the boardwalk at Atlantic City while his dad gambled all day and all night at the casino. One thing was certain, Jack's dad always ensured that the rent was paid and that the refrigerator and pantry were stocked full with food before he would take the rest of the money to go gamble with. Jack swore that he would never get into gambling because he saw how it affected his family. However, when he turned 21, he found himself in the throes of a gambling addiction that landed him into some very heavy debt. He had several credit cards and a couple of high interest rate loans that he used to finance his bad gambling habit. Jack kept his gambling debt a secret from Karen when they first met because he was embarrassed by it. Karen didn't find out about it until after they were married. It became a huge stress on their marriage. For Jack, gambling was a sensation and rush that provided him comfort in moments of stress and vulnerability. His game of choice was blackjack. It was his poison. Some of his darkest hours were on the blackjack table at the casino. One moment in particular was when he took Karen on a road trip to Atlantic City. Karen was pregnant with Hannah at the time. Jack and Karen had gotten up at the crack of dawn to take a little trip from Quantico to Atlantic City. It was to be a fun trip for the both of them. Jack wanted to show Karen some of the places he and his family would stop at on their way to Atlantic City. He also wanted her to experience the boardwalk and to share his adventures with her from when he was a kid. It was a great trip until Jack decided to try his luck on the blackjack table. He was there all night and into the early morning hours. Fed up with his gambling, Karen thought to herself, "I know Jack wouldn't let me walk back to the car by myself at 1:30 in the morning, especially with me being pregnant with our child." Testing to see what Jack would do, Karen walked up to him and asked for the keys to the car; and before she could even blink, Jack reached into his pocket and handed her the keys. Stunned with disbelief that Jack had no hesitation to allow her to walk to the car at that time of the morning in an unsafe and unfamiliar neighborhood, Karen was furious! Immediately she thought, "How could he?!" She ended up taking the keys from him but staying in the casino lobby until he was finished losing all of their money. This wasn't the first time nor was it the last time that Jack would gamble. He struggled with his gambling addiction for the early part of their marriage. If it weren't for God giving her the patience, Karen would have divorced him years ago.

Jack found the strength and fortitude in God to overcome the temptation to gamble after he became a Christian. It wasn't an overnight fix for him. From time to time the temptation to gamble would rear its ugly head, and Jack would find the courage and strength in Christ to resist and overcome. Little by little, moment-by-moment, day-by-day, year-by-year, as Jack grew in his Christian faith, he learned to trust in God's presence and power to overcome the temptation. His spiritual growth was a testimony of his new life of devotion to God. This new life was characterized by meaning, fulfillment, love, joy, and peace. He got to this place in his life by the grace of God and by implementing some spiritual rhythms in his life that consisted of practical things like attending church where he learned to pray, read the Bible, worship God, fellowship with other Christians, and serve others. His outlook on life changed as he grew in faith. His Christian faith became an integral part of who he was and how he lived. He grew stronger and learned to live victoriously in God's power to overcome the temptations he faced. The temptations that tried to lure him back into the dark places that only brought destruction in his life. God took the dark and ugly times in Jack's life and turned them into beauty and light.

Jack began to feel the irresistible urge to gamble as he got closer to "Sin City." The old evil friend came courting. It knocked on his door. He couldn't ignore or deny it. It had an irresistible draw. It was like an itch that needed to be scratched. It invited him to a place of escape. It would be a place that he could go and self-medicate. It was a place where time stood still for a moment, and where he could get off of life's carousel of hurt and pain. He felt like he needed to get off. He wanted to get off of this crazy ride of grief and mourning.

Jack was at a crossroads. He could either keep on driving or stop in Las Vegas. The temptation was overwhelming, and he found himself taking the exit onto Dunes Road/West Flamingo Road. Before he knew it, Jack was on the Vegas Strip and trying to find parking at Caesars Palace.

Jack made his way into the casino entrance and immediately withdrew a couple hundred dollars from the first ATM he found which so happen to be conveniently located everywhere. Still fighting the urge to gamble, Jack sat at the first blackjack table he saw. In the back of his mind, Jack knew he shouldn't be there. He felt like he had to constantly be looking over his shoulder to see if someone he knew would catch him there. As he dismissed the thoughts, he placed the two hundred dollar bills on the table to play. Jack could feel the butterflies in his stomach coupled with the adrenaline surging through his body. It was a hauntingly familiar feeling for him. The dealer held up the hundred dollar bills to the light to visibly inspect them, and then ran a counterfeit detector pen over each of them as a second means of verification. She then counted out two hundred dollars in casino chips in front of her and then called out to the pit boss, "Changing two hundred." Then she gently pushed the chips over to Jack and said, "Good luck."

Jack pulled the chips close to him on the table, took twenty dollars in chips and placed them on the betting spot in front of him. The dealer began to deal the cards out of the dealing shoe. Jack's first card was a queen of hearts followed by a two of clubs. "Twelve," he thought to himself. The dealer's face up card was a king of spades. Jack instinctively began to shuffle the small stack of the chips in front of him with his right hand; it was a player's trick he had learned back when he use to gamble. He could hear the chips rattle against each other as he shuffled them. There was an indescribable sensation in how the texture of the chips felt against his fingers. The felt material that lined the blackjack table under his fingertips accentuated the sensation. Now Jack started feeling the "rush" that he had long forgotten since the last time he was ever on a blackjack table. The instincts all came back to him like it was just yesterday. The dealer looked to him for his move. Jack tapped the table lightly just inches behind his cards to signify that he wanted to hit. The dealer dealt him an eight of clubs. "Twenty," Jack thought. Then he waved his right hand over his cards signifying that he wanted to stay. The dealer flipped over the hole card showing a nine of diamonds. "Nineteen," Jack thought immediately as he added the cards in his head. He won. The dealer paid out twenty dollars in chips to him, and he stacked it on top of his current bet to make it forty dollars. The dealer began the next round by dealing Jack a seven of hearts and then a four of clubs. She showed a six of diamonds for her face up card. Jack knew instinctively to double down, so he put out forty more dollars in chips next to his original bet, and the dealer dealt his card faced down. She then flipped over her hole card showing a jack of clubs. "Sixteen," Jack thought to himself, "She's going to bust." She deals herself a four of diamonds. "Twenty." Then she flips over Jack's double down card to reveal a jack of hearts. "Twenty-one." Another win for Jack. It only was a matter of time that all the cares in the world. All the burdens in Jack's heart succumbed to the "fix" of his gambling addiction that made everything else fade away. The fix that his addiction provided him was an escape from reality. It was the medicine and antidote for whatever hurt or pain he was feeling. For Jack, it was the hurt and pain of loss. But as quickly as those wins came that pulled him into the escape so did the losses come that brought him back to reality. Within thirty minutes, Jack had lost all of his chips.

His natural instinct was to return to the ATM to grab more money. So he got off of the blackjack table and went back to the ATM. As he was pulling out his debit card from his wallet, he suddenly came to his senses and thought to himself, "What in the heck am I doing?" In just a moment, he was pulled out of his place of escape and back into reality. He put his debit card back into his wallet and his wallet back into his pocket and walked away.

As Jack made his way out of the gaming area, the faces of the people in the crowd that past on his left and right were just a blur as he tried to make some kind of sense to what just happened. As he walked through the halls of the Caesars Palace, he felt completely empty and numb, but it was strangely a different kind of numbness and emptiness than what he felt at Karen's funeral. It was an eerie numbness that was deteriorating to his soul. And it was a ghostly emptiness that was deeply hollow and void of any breath or life. Then out of the blue, he found himself standing in front of an exact replica of Michelangelo's Renaissance sculpture of the biblical character David at the Appian Way Shops in Caesars Palace. Upon looking at the sculpture of David, Jack was reminded of David's words in the Bible from 2 Samuel 22:29 "...the LORD turns my darkness into light." David was reflecting on how God had taken some of the most disparaging moments in his life and turned them into something wonderful. We use the term "darkness" metaphorically to describe some of the most evil, ugliest, disparaging, anguishing, painful, embarrassing, and disheartening moments that we face in our lives. They are times and predicaments where we have acted in selfishness, greed, envy, jealousy, bitterness, unforgiveness, and hatred. They are times when we struggled with loss, abuse, or addiction that causes us to feel guilt and shame. But God can turn that darkness into light. God can take the most darkest, desperate and hopeless of situations and turn them into something divinely magnificent and majestically beautiful.[3] God can turn our darkest hour into the light of His glory. King David was a prime example of that. Though he was esteemed throughout history, David had his moments of darkness.

As Jack stood there staring up into the face of the sculpture of David, he just happened to notice a dapper and well-dressed stranger on the other side of the sculpture staring back at him. "He looked like a whale," (a Vegas' term for a high roller), Jack thought.

The stranger approached Jack and said, "Looks like you lost."

"You can't even imagine," Jack replied in anguish.

"Oh I definitely can. I lost over $10,000 tonight in less than an hour."

"I lost more than that," said Jack as if he were competing. But his loss was in reference to Karen.

"Well, I recently lost my fiancée because she couldn't deal with my gambling, so she broke up with me."

"I'm sorry to hear that," Jack said as he looked up at the statue in front of them.

"Well, it is what it is. But look at me now. I'm free as a bird. I cashed out everything I owned and even sold my car. I bought a bus ticket to this town and wagered it all. I hit a really good streak and have been living it large here for the past week. The $10,000 I mentioned earlier was only a drop in the bucket compared to what I won a few days ago. The casino "comped" (another Vegas' term for complimentary or offered for free) me a room and all of my meals in this place for the past week. I've been living it up man!"

"Was it worth losing your fiancée over?" Jack asked sarcastically.

"It is what it is man. I can't complain with the life I'm living now."

For whatever reason, it was hard for Jack to believe him. Jack was feeling empty inside, but this random stranger appeared empty in a worse way but didn't realize it. His finely tailored suit, patent leather shoes, expensive watch and jewelry were only a façade that hid a soul deep within that was empty and full of darkness. Jack could sense that there was a hurt within this man that was completely different than the hurt Jack was feeling from his loss of Karen.

Then two scantily clad extremely young beautiful ladies came up to the stranger, and put their arms around him simultaneously. One of them said coyly, "Hey baby, we finally picked out the necklaces we want." While the other continued flirtatiously, "You ready to get them for us like you promised?"

"Well, I got to go take care of some business with my lady friends. Good luck."

As the stranger left, Jack remembered how his brother, like this stranger, also lost his fiancée because of gambling. But now his brother is happily married to a new girl he met at church after he quit gambling and turned his life around. He also remembered something his brother had said to him a while back. Jack's brother also overcame the addiction of gambling after he became a Christian. He once told Jack that if he ever lost his wife, he wouldn't know what he would do. He told Jack that he was afraid that he would most likely resort back to gambling in order to numb the pain of such a loss. The only thing that would keep him from going back to gambling is his three young kids. Immediately Jack pulled out his cellphone and called his brother. He wasn't sure why he did. Maybe Jack was looking for empathy. Perhaps it was for encouragement. Possibly it could have been for advice. Or maybe it was to hear the sound of someone who would understand what he had just done. His brother answered, "What's up Jack? How are you doing?"

"I'm in Vegas," replied Jack.

"What are you doing there?" his brother asked concerned.

"What do you think?" Jack replied disappointed.

"How much?" asked his brother knowing Jack probably gambled and most likely lost.

"A couple of hundred, but that's not the point."

"I know," respond his brother.

Jack shared with his brother about how he bought an RV and about his plans to drive up north to clear his head and possibly to start anew.

He explained how he had this uncontrollable urge to pull over in Las Vegas to gamble.

"I know what you're feeling and going through, and I understand how gambling can be a painkiller," said his brother empathetically. "I know you're going through a lot of pain right now."

Jack asked, "What should I do now?"

His brother replied, "What would Karen want you to do?"

"I don't know. All I know is that my heart aches," cried Jack. "It hurts so bad. I miss her so much. Why did she have to go?" he questioned as tears began to run down his face.

"I understand that it is a time for you to mourn, but it is also a time to rejoice knowing that Karen is in heaven with the Lord," his brother reminded him. "She is in the best place that she could ever be and with the best Person that she could ever be with. She is in a place and with a Person that her heart and soul were created for and has always longed for. So rejoice for her by moving forward. That's what she would want for you to do. I know it's difficult now, but let your heart rejoice for her, and there you will find your healing and hope."

"I know," replied Jack. "You're right."

Jack knew that what his brother said was absolute true. It was the premise behind his favorite Bible passage from John 14:1-4. Jack knew that each of us where made for a place and for a Person. That place is heaven and that Person is Jesus Christ. There is no better place to be and no better person to be with. Karen was in good hands, and so was Jack.

Jack's brother prayed for him before they got off the phone. Jack thanked him for his prayer and his understanding.

As Jack began to leave, he noticed the plaque that was affixed to the base of the replica sculpture of Michelangelo's David that read:

David is an exact replica of Michelangelo's masterpiece, hewn in the early 16th Century. He stands 18 feet high and weighs more than nine tons. He was sculpted from the same Italian marble used by the master for the original. David's pose depicts the tense moment, of tightening muscles and rising excitement, just before his facing and slaying the towering Goliath.

Jack was encouraged by those words as he remembered that God was always going to be with him as He was with David that day he faced the towering giant Goliath. God had slayed many giants in Jack's life, and Jack was certain that the giant of having to live without Karen was going to be defeated with God by his side.

Jack made his way out of the casino and back to his RV. He drove out of the parking structure and back onto the interstate. As he was leaving Las Vegas, he caught a glimpse of the city lights in his left side rear view mirror. The Sky Beam from the Luxor Hotel once again caught his eye. Jack found it interesting how it was the only light that pointed northward. For him, it was a subtle yet divine reminder of the heavenly direction towards the place and Person he ought to be setting his sights on.

For we live by faith, not by sight.

2 Corinthians 5:7

CHAPTER 5
Nomads and Sojourners

Jack was amazed by the view as he drove through the northwestern tip of Arizona. Although Jack had never been to the Grand Canyon, he felt like he had just experienced a miniature version of it. Jack always wanted to take Karen to the Grand Canyon, especially when she earned her graduate degree from Grand Canyon University. Ironically, the university campus was not anywhere near the Grand Canyon; instead, it was located in Phoenix. During Karen's graduation, Jack thought that they could make a quick trip to the Grand Canyon. The only downside was that the Grand Canyon was three and half hours out of their way. So they never made it out.

In crossing the Arizona and Utah state line, Jack found himself engulfed by a caravan of Volkswagen camper vans. Jack had always been enamored by the camper van lifestyle. He followed a young couple on YouTube who documents their life on the road as they lived out of their camper van. Their nomadic lifestyle was something that always had a yearning in Jack's heart. Seeing the opportunity to possibly observe them in real life was exciting for Jack, so he accelerated on the gas pedal to keep up with them.

Jack followed behind them trying to remain as inconspicuous as possible. The caravan turned off of the interstate and headed towards the town of Hurricane, Utah. As Jack continued to follow closely behind, he found himself at the entrance to Sand Hallow State Park. The camper vans filed into the park one by one after paying their entrance fees. Jack pulled up to the check-in station and kindly asked the park ranger where the caravan was headed. The ranger informed him that they all were headed to the South Shore Primitive Camping Area on the beach. Jack asked the ranger what and where that area was. She explained to him that it was a plot of land in the state park that surrounded the reservoir. The beach was not a real beach but the reservoir itself. Campers are allowed to park and set up their campsites anywhere along the beach. She advised Jack to stay on the gravel and keep out of the soft sand in that particular area. She explained to him how vehicles in the past would often get stuck in the soft sand and would have to call for assistance to get towed out. She also informed Jack that the park services had no utilities to assist him in the event he were to get stuck. She warned Jack that if he did get stuck that he would have to call for services outside of the state park and pay for any tow charges himself. Jack kept that in mind as he paid the $15 primitive camping fee for the night and proceeded to catch up to the caravan as he head towards their campsite.

Jack arrived at a quaint secluded spot just before dawn. The area was right on the reservoir that could have easily been mistaken for as a natural lake. Soft orange sand blanketed the entire site where gravel pushed up from the surface in some areas. Lush green stalks of grass protruded from the perimeter waters of the reservoir as the mountain range served as a stunning backdrop that completely surrounded the area. The view of the surrounding desert was amazingly majestic.

As the sun began to set, the caravan of camper vans synchronously parked in a circle formation that looked like a caravan of gypsy wagons. It was obvious that this was not the first time they've done this. Jack on the other hand parked Johnny B at a distance as not to intrude in on their gathering.

In no time at all, the camper vans had their site fully set up. Their setup consisted of van awnings staked to the ground, popped up camper shells, lawn chairs out, and a campfire up and blazing. Some of them were preparing dinner on the stovetops that were equipped inside of their camper vans while others were firing up portable gas grills under the open sky. It wasn't long before the smell of burning charcoal and the aroma of grilled meat filled the air.

As Jack sat enjoying and admiring the carefree nomadic lifestyle of the campers, it dawned on him that he was now sharing in this same lifestyle as well. He was free from the cares of and responsibilities that kept him settled down to one place. He was free to roam the land. He could get up and go to bed at any time. His front yard could be the sands of a shoreline, the forest of a national park, or the snow of a mountain range. Nothing kept him bound. He was free to wander and settle wherever he wished.

It didn't take long for the folks in the caravan to notice Jack sitting in front of his RV all by himself. One of the young men, possibly in his late twenties, approached Jack. He had dirty-blonde hair that was a little past shoulder length. He was wearing a tank top, cargo shorts, flip-flops, and a baseball cap that he wore backwards.

"Hi, my name is Conrad. We couldn't help but notice that you're all by yourself over here, and we wanted to know if you would like to join us for some dinner around the fire."

Trying desperately to contain his excitement, Jack said nonchalantly, "Sure. I'd like that. My name is Jack." Jack grabbed his lawn chair and followed Conrad over to their campsite where he sat with everyone around the fire.

"Everyone, this Jack. Jack, this is everyone," said Conrad as he introduced Jack.

"Hi everyone. Thank you for the invitation. I look forward to meeting you all before the night ends," Jack said with a smile as he burst with excitement within.

"I'm Leonard. What brings you out here Jack?" one of the campers asked.

"I'm actually trying my wits at your lifestyle," replied Jack.

"How long have you been living in your RV now?" asked Leonard.

"I just started a couple of days ago," smiled Jack.

"You won't regret it," assured Leonard. "Glad to see you made the choice."

"Not sure if I actually made the choice but rather the choice was made for me," quipped Jack.

"Regardless, I'm glad you're out here and glad to make your acquaintance Jack," added Conrad. "This is my wife Esther and our dog Fifty-cent."

"That's a unique name," Jack said curiously.

"Actually, Esther is a quite common name," joked Conrad. "We named our dog Fifty-cent after the rapper."

"Oh, I get it! I've heard of him, but I'm not familiar with his music. How long have you all been doing this for?" Jack asked.

Each couple was more than excited to respond to Jack's question. One of the couples had been living out of their camper van for just six months. Another couple had been doing it for almost a year now. One of the couples had been doing it for almost two years, and Conrad and Esther had been on the road for over three years.

"Three years?" Jack asked as his eyes widened.

"Yup," replied Conrad as he looked over to Esther.

Fascinated by the longevity of each of their stints living out on the open road, Jack was filled with questions. He asked how they made the decision to leave everything behind and hit the road, how they worked and made a living, how they sustain themselves, take showers, use the bathroom, and any other challenges they faced. After hours of entertaining Jack's questions, most of the couples retired for the evening except for Conrad and Esther. They continued to chat with Jack.

"So what was it for you guys? What made you decided to hit the open roads?" asked Jack.

Conrad explained how he and Esther initially started the adventure as an experiment at the beginning of 2013 to discover whether it was possible to live such a lifestyle while working remotely. In their quest, it had become more about a life of simplicity, freedom, and truth.

"We've had our share of ups and downs," Conrad explained, "But we've never regretted our decision nor do we plan to give it up."

"We've met so many wonderful fellow nomads along the way," Conrad continued, "And we've just continued to embrace the unknown and follow our passions."

"What was the biggest decision you had to make in order to make this dream of yours happen?" Jack asked.

"Just simply taking the plunge," replied Conrad. "The biggest challenge is jumping off the edge and right into it."

It sounded all too familiar for Jack. Their story reminded him of the Hebrew people from the Book of Numbers 13:26-33. It was a time after the Lord God had delivered them out of slavery in Egypt and brought them out to the desert towards the Promised Land. According to the Bible, it was a land flowing with milk and honey. The Israelites eventually came to a place in the wilderness called Kadesh in the Desert of Paran that sat on the border just outside of the Promised Land. The Hebrew people sent out spies into the land to see whether they were capable of overcoming the odds that they would face. The spies returned and reported that there were giants in the land and that the Hebrew people looked like mere grasshoppers compared to the giants. These were the words of the spies from Numbers 13:32-33:

> *The land we explored devours those living in it. All the people we saw there are great size. We saw the Nephilim there (the descendants of Anak come from the Nephilim). We seemed like grasshoppers in our own eyes, and we looked the same to them.*

The perception was that the giants viewed the Hebrew people as small weak grasshoppers, which lead them to accept that perception of themselves. They had a choice whether to cower in fear of the giants or step forward in faith into the Promised Land despite the opposition. God promised the land to them. He also promised that He would not leave them but be by their side. The Hebrew people stood at a crossroads; it was a place of decision. Were they going to trust God and move forward in the face of uncertainty and overwhelming obstacles? Or would they succumb to their fear? When you come to a crossroads in your life where you are faced with a choice between doubt due to overwhelming odds or faith in God, always choose faith.[5]

The story in the Book of Numbers 13 was so indicative of the choice that Conrad and Esther had made in choosing to live the nomadic lifestyle. It was about stepping out in faith or as Conrad put it, "taking the plunge or jumping off." The interesting thing about the story in the Book of Numbers 13 is that despite how God was with the Hebrew people, they still viewed themselves as small weak grasshoppers. Because coincidentally in the Book of Isaiah 40:22 it reveals to us that God sees all the inhabitants of the earth as grasshoppers. Though the Hebrew people saw themselves as grasshoppers compared to the giants in the Promised Land, God saw the giants in the land as grasshoppers to Him. What a stark contrast. God was on the side of the Hebrews, and He promised them a land where they could live in freedom and promise. The Book of Romans 8:31 tells us that if God is for us then who or even what can be against us. We have to believe and have faith that God is not only with us but that He is also for us. We should not curtail our faith in God despite the overwhelming obstacles we face in life that causes us to fear and doubt. We make either the choice to cower in fear or step out in faith and trust in God. Unfortunately the Israelites chose fear rather than faith. It was that fear that prevented them from entering into the Promised Land and ended up wandering in the wilderness for 40 years. Only those who had faith in God entered into the Promised Land.

Conrad and Esther took a step of faith towards freedom and passion. Faith is far greater and more powerful when it is placed in Christ. Great and wonderful opportunities await us in the unknown. It will take a step of faith in God for those opportunities to present themselves to us. Fear and doubt are obstacles that prevent us from taking steps of faith. Fear will only pave a path to regret. Do not allow fear to steal away great and wonderful possibilities for your life. God loves us. He has a wonderful and prosperous plan and future in store for us. He is always for us. We have to put our faith in Him and step out.

The star-filled sky radiated with brilliance as the campfire slowly began to dissipate into glowing embers. Jack painted word pictures of a life characterized by faith. It was a life of freedom and adventure echoed from a hunger deep within Jack's soul. Everyday provided an invitation towards faith in God. Jack knew that the hunger deep within him could only be satiated by God. But it required Jack to step out and take the plunge in faith. Living by faith everyday was an adventure in itself filled with opportunities to step out and take the plunge. It was an exciting life that pressed towards a destination towards the heavenly.

Jack made one last comment to Conrad and Esther before making a gesture to retire back to his RV for the evening. He explained to them how he personally felt that we are all sojourners and nomads here on earth. And though we have the opportunity to enjoy the journey, deep within each of our souls longs for a home we will not find on this side of heaven.

Jack stood up, folded up his lawn chair, thanked Conrad and Esther for their kindness and hospitality, and made his way back to Johnny B. As he crawled into bed that evening, he said a little prayer and thanked God for bringing him across this little group of kindhearted folks that reminded him how much we are all sojourners and nomads not yet home.

He gives strength to the weary and increases the power of the weak.

Isaiah 40:29

CHAPTER 6
Mirror Mirror on the Wall

Many of the couples from the previous night were still fast asleep. The smoldering campfire smoke from the previous night billowed into the cool brisk morning air as the sunrise barely peeked through the horizon. Jack got up to brush his teeth, for he couldn't stay in bed any longer. Afterwards, he headed back towards the interstate.

Coffee was the only thing on Jack's mind this early in the morning. He took the next exit in search of the nearest coffeehouse. As he entered into Cedar City, he found a quaint little storefront café off of Main Street called the Grind Coffeehouse. It received four out of five stars on Yelp with 74 reviews, so it was a joint worth checking out.

The café had a few small tables outside along the sidewalk. Christmas lights and small flags from different countries laced the awning above the entrance.

The interior of the café had a cozy eclectic décor that invoked feelings of warmth and comfort. The coffee bar style counter with the typical blackboard chalk written menu consisted of an array of breakfast sandwiches and gourmet coffee drinks. As Jack stood in line to place his order, he couldn't help but notice the different flooring surfaces in the café that ranged from tile, to carpet, to a raised vinyl covered stage that housed a lacquer white baby grand piano. Perhaps the coffeehouse featured local musicians during the evening hours. The ceiling had exposed air ducts and two small retro chrome ceiling fans. The fans had three tubular lights that extended from the center that made them look like mini spaceships landing on earth in an alien invasion movie.

The seating in the café was a collection of old school 50s diner tables, wooden dining room tables, a variety of couches, and plush armchairs. The café provided an entrance to the bookstore next door. Original paintings that resembled cracked white wall plaster hung on the wall, and the area around the paintings was corded off just like in a museum. It has often been said that art is in the eye of the beholder.

Jack was surely not one to judge what would be considered real art, but instead appreciated the paintings because his undergraduate degree was in art with a focus on painting. The rest of the walls were decorated with a myriad of nostalgic photographs and memorabilia.

After taking in all of the interesting décor in the café, Jack decided to order the "All Day Breakfast Sandwich" that contained eggs, chili peppers, onions, tomatoes, and spinach with a side of bacon, and a cappuccino. Jack loved the foam in cappuccinos; it was his favorite part of the coffee. Jack took a seat next to a mirror that hung on the wall that read, "See The Possibilities." Sitting next to him was a slender old man with silver grey hair wearing a long sleeve army green crew neck tee, khaki cargo pants, and a pair of grey Crocs sandals. He had headphones on that were connected to his laptop computer. He appeared to be listening to something on his laptop. Jack thought that he was either listening to music or watching videos on YouTube. Jack leaned over to catch a glimpse of the man's computer screen. He appeared to be doing homework online. Jack recognized the online application that the old man was using. The application was called Blackboard which is an online learning management system typically used by colleges and universities for their online programs. The older man caught Jack's prying eyes, so he pulled off his headphones and greeted Jack as if to query him regarding his curiosity.

"I'm sorry," Jack responded a little embarrassed having been caught looking over.

"No worries," replied the old man.

"I couldn't help but notice that you have Blackboard up on your laptop and wondered what class you're taking."

"Actually, I'm teaching one online," replied the man.

"Oh really," Jack replied back excitedly, "I use to teach online as well."

"Where at?" asked the old man.

"Crown College."

"Oh yeah, I'm familiar with Crown. That's the little private Christian college in Minnesota right?"

"Yes," Jack replied surprised that he knew about Crown College. "How about yourself? Where do you teach?"

"Ashford University."

"Oh really, I have a couple of friends and family who got their degrees from Ashford."

"If you don't mind me asking, what do you teach?" Jack asked.

"Psychology," replied the old man.

"My wife had interest in getting into that field of study, but she eventually finished her degree in communications. She was such a great counselor, I was hoping she would eventually get her Psy.D."

"Yeah, I got mine at Baylor," replied the old man.

"Baylor? Wow! I'm impressed," said Jack.

"How about yourself?" asked the man.

"I got my Ph.D. at Regent University in organizational leadership with a major in church leadership. I use to teach an online class call "Concept of Global and Ethical Leadership" as an adjunct professor for Crown College. I also taught some graduate level Christian ministry courses."

Jack's order was ready, so he briefly excused himself to grab his breakfast sandwich and coffee and then sat back down at the table next to the man.

"Oh by the way, my name is Jack," as he extended out his hand.

"Jim," replied the man as he shook Jack's hand and smiled.

"How long have you been teaching now?" Jack asked.

"35 years."

"Wow! That's a long time. All 35 years online?" asked Jack.

"No, I use to be on faculty at Utah State University in my earlier days," replied Jim. "What got you into teaching?"

"It's a long story," said Jack as he took a bite of his breakfast sandwich.

"I'm not going anywhere," replied Jim as he leaned back in his chair suggesting that he was interested in hearing Jack's story.

"I use to pastor a church," Jack began. "And after 10 years, I was getting frustrated with how things were going. More specifically how the church wasn't growing. I considered quitting the ministry and getting into teaching. So the next step was to get my Ph.D. so that I could teach at the university level. That's how I came across the program at Regent University. Going back to school turned out to be a blessing in disguise. My doctoral work and research provided me with a new and insightful perspective that eventually renewed my passion for ministry and pastoring in a small church context.

"So you're no longer pastoring?" asked Jim.

"No," replied Jack. "I retired a couple of years ago."

"Are you still teaching as a professor?"

"Not anymore, I stopped teaching when my wife was diagnosed with cancer. She passed away recently."

"I'm sorry to hear that Jack," said Jim sympathetically. "So what do you do now?"

Jack took a moment to think and then replied, "Nothing really. I'm retired. I guess that makes me done."

"Done with what?" Jim asked.

"Done with ministry, done with teaching, done with whatever else I guess."

"Do you think God is done with you?" Jim asked with a slight rhetorical tone. "Yes Jack, I believe in God. I'm a Christian too," as he smiled at Jack reassuring him that he understands what it's like to live having faith in Christ.

After thinking for a moment, Jack remembered that Jim did mention that he graduated from Baylor University, which should have given him a clue that Jim might have been a Christian too.

Jim then proceeded to share with Jack how Moses died at the age of 120, yet the most profound ministry that God accomplished through Moses was in the last 40 years of his life. The Book of Deuteronomy 34:7 says that when Moses died, his eyesight was undimmed and his vigor was unabated. Moses lived his life to the very end with the vision and passion for the things of God. God gives each of us a vision and passion for our lives. God-given visions, dreams, goals, and aspirations must be seen through the eyes of faith. They are far bigger than ourselves. They are God-sized. They require us to live in God's strength, power, and resources through faith. The Bible says that we should walk by faith and not by sight. Oftentimes what we see and know in the natural can deter and discourage us from greater things that God has in store for us. We have to see it through the eyes of faith. We have to see it and imagine it differently. The Bible also says that God will help us accomplish greater things beyond our capacity. God is faithful to see us through the times when we are weak, tired, exhausted, and ready to give up. We need God's supernatural strength to help us achieve those God-given visions, dreams, goals, and aspirations. The Bible is filled with great promises of God's plans for each of our lives. The Book of Jeremiah 29:11 tells us that those plans that God has for us are plans to prosper us, not to harm us, to give us a future and a hope.

We might think we are done, but God still has wonderful plans and things to accomplish. Oftentimes we'll either retire or give up, but we still have a lot more of life to live. God's good plan on earth continues to unfold every single day of our lives, and we each have the wonderful privilege and opportunity to be a part of that plan. Even when we think we're done, God is not done. He has wonderful things still in store for us just around the bend despite where we are in life. Oftentimes when we feel like the odds are stacked against us, and there's no hope we give up and throw in the towel. When we feel like there is no more fight left in us, we quit. When all seems lost, we throw our hands up in surrender. When things look bleak in the natural and you feel weak and helpless, see it differently through the eyes of faith and trust that God will see you through to the very end.[6]

Jack already knew everything Jim had shared with him. He had preached out of this passage of the Book of Deuteronomy with practically the exact same message. He would encourage his congregation never to give up on God regardless of how long He may take. God allows our circumstances and predicaments to play out in our lives in a way that provides us opportunities to discover Him more. The more we discover God, the more we discover ourselves in light of the truth of God. God sustains us in His great power and strength in our weakness. God gives us hope to see a better tomorrow.

Jack knew that despite Moses' old age, God gave Moses vision and strength to accomplish the task of bringing God's people into the Promised Land. For Jack, it was humbling to hear a message that he once preached to his congregation now coming from someone else. It was a gentle reminder from God that He was not done with Jack yet.

Maybe it was Karen's passing that made Jack think he was done. When Karen was diagnosed with cancer, Jack retired from the pastorate and resigned from his teaching position in order to be there for Karen. It was the toughest thing they had ever gone through in all of their marriage. Karen was as healthy as an ox. She was always exercising and eating right. Health and nutrition was very important to her. She was always after Jack about his health and particularly his bad eating habits. If it weren't for Karen, Jack would probably never make a doctor's appointment. Karen was the one who ensured that they both got their annual physical check-ups.

Cancer is an ugly disease and discriminates against no one. Jack felt like the wind was knocked out of him when they received Karen's prognosis. It sapped the life out of him. It was like he couldn't see straight nor get out of bed in the mornings. Every morning seemed like a bad dream that he would have to live another day in. Jack had sympathy pains in that he was as physically weak as the cancer made Karen, but she remained strong to the end. Karen had so much faith in God despite what she was going through. She was so close to God because of her faith. Her love for God was so evident in the way she lived and in the way she loved. Karen had a relationship with God that Jack was extremely jealous of. Jack didn't know anyone as close to God the same way that Karen was. The vision that God had given to her for her life was undimmed, and though her strength deteriorated from the cancer, her resolve to love and trust God was unabated. Karen's favorite Bible verse was Jeremiah 29:11. She knew God's good plans for her life, and she completely trusted Him with her life through the entire ordeal. She knew God was good, and His good plan would unfold for her life despite the cancer. Karen understood that the ordeal of her condition was a test of her faith in God. She didn't understand why it happened. There were times when she questioned God; but in the end, it only resulted in her faith growing stronger. Jack was amazed at how strong Karen's faith was to the very end. She fought to the very end. She fought the good fight of faith. And then God took her. When Jack lost Karen, the vision God had given him for his life and ministry dimmed and his strength and resolve abated.

Jim pointed to the mirror that hung up on the wall and told Jack, "Look in the mirror and see the possibilities that still lie ahead. Stay the course Jack. God is not done with you my friend."

"Thank you for the reminder Jim," Jack humbly replied.

"Do you mind if I pray for you Jack?" asked Jim.

"I would be honored if you did," Jack answered.

Jim laid his hand upon Jack's shoulder and bowed his head as he prayed for Jack. The words of Jim's prayer were simple yet elegant certain that God was listening and that He would eventually answer. It was a prayer of faith.

Afterwards, Jack thanked Jim for praying for him. It gave Jack a resolve to envision the possibilities that still lay ahead for him. Jack was humbled that this old professor took the time to take him back to school again.

But godliness with contentment is great gain.

1 Timothy 6:6

CHAPTER 7
All This And Jesus Too

As Jack made his way northward, the small beautiful mountain ranges that looked like postcards of the Grand Canyon were replaced by flat farmland. Alfalfa blanketed the landscape as far as the eye could see. Bales of hay were scattered throughout the fields on both sides of the interstate. Many of the bales were rectangular in shape while others were rolled up like carpet.

From the interstate, Jack spotted a golf course. A little puzzled and in complete shock, he did not expect to see a golf course out in the middle of nowhere. He assumed that Utah had golf courses but didn't think he would see one right off of the interstate. Full of curiosity, Jack immediately took the next exit right into Fillmore. As he entered the small rural town, he saw the sign for Paradise Golf Resort. There wasn't anything extravagant about the resort unlike some of the courses that Jack was accustomed to playing. He and his brother use to play some of the most expensive courses in San Diego and in the San Francisco Bay area. For Jack, it was all about how nice the course was and whether or not the pro shop carried ball markers for sale. Jack had a thing about collecting ball markers from each of the courses he played at. Ball markers are small magnetic nickel-size tokens that had the golf courses name or logo on it. The markers are used to mark your golf ball on the putting green when you have to move your ball out of the way for another golfer. Jack collected them as souvenirs. He would never play a course that didn't sell personalized ball markers with the course's name or logo on it. He believed that a course that didn't sell personalized ball markers was not a course worth playing. Most high-end resort type courses sold them. Jack had a collection of over seven dozen ball markers from the various golf courses where he played.

Jack noticed that the clubhouse for the golf course was located on the backside of a Best Western motel. A dozen golf carts filled the motel's parking lot. With it's green metal awning, held up by green wooden pillars that were attached to a green metal banister, and the green patio floor that was lined with that green carpet-like material resembling green grass on the surface of a putting green, you would have thought that the clubhouse had a St. Patrick's Day themed decor. Walking up the catwalk that lead to the clubhouse, Jack noticed a middle-aged brunette woman pleasantly sitting at a black iron-grate table on the clubhouse patio. She appeared to be doing some work on her laptop computer.

"Well hello," she greeted Jack with a big smile.

"Hello, I'm Jack. I saw the golf course from the interstate."

"My name is Liz," as she got up from her seat to grab a scorecard from inside which she handed to Jack. "The course is a 9-hole executive course. The course was privately owned by a local farmer even though it was attached to the Best Western next door. We're not busy, so I get can you on the course right now if you'd like. Green fees are $15," explained Liz anticipating that Jack stopped by to play.

"Oh," Jack chuckled. "I don't have my clubs with me."

"We rent clubs," Liz said as if to solve that problem.

Jack really would have loved to play. He prefers playing 9-hole executive courses. He always thought that the 18-hole full-length course was way too long to play. A typical 18-hole course can take anywhere from three to four hours to play with a friend, and a full foursome can take up to five or even six hours if the course is busy. "As much as I would love to play, I don't think right now is a good time," Jack said disappointingly.

"Anytime is a good time to play golf," chimed Liz.

"You're absolutely right," assured Jack, "But I was just curious when I saw the course from the interstate and wanted to check it out. Do you mind if I just sat here for a little bit?"

"Not at all," Liz said invitingly.

Jack took a seat at the black iron-grate table next to Liz's and stared out over the course. It was a little warm that afternoon, but the shade provided by the clubhouse awning, coupled with a slight breeze, made the weather tolerable. The humble scenery overlooking the course's 9th hole was a peaceful sight despite the traffic noise from the interstate.

"Are you originally from here?" Jack asked as he looked over to Liz.

"No," replied Liz, "I originally grew up near San Francisco."

"So how long have you lived in Fillmore?" asked Jack.

"Oh, let's see, since I was married 33 years ago," she replied.

"Did you meet your husband here?"

"No. I actually met him when we were attending Utah State."

"What does he do?"

"He's a farmer."

"What does he farm?"

"Alfalfa, hay, however you see it. He also raises cattle."

"Any kids," inquired Jack.

"I have four kids and 10 grandkids."

"Wow! 10 grandkids?! You don't look old enough to have 10 grandkids," replied Jack as he thought about Hannah and Jimmy. Jack shared with Liz that he only has a daughter and a grandson. They went on about their kids and grandkids. When the conversation started to die down, Jack asked, "Any place in town that you'd recommend to grab a bite to eat?"

Liz pointed down the road and told Jack that there's a really neat place called Cluff's Carhop Café. There were other places in town, but Cluff's was a unique and a definite spot for any visitor to hit up. Jack asked her what she typically orders there. She recommended their Chicken Malibu.

"Thanks for the recommendation," said Jack. "I will definitely check it out."

Before Jack got up to leave, Liz warned him that the people who worked there were a bit peculiar. She explained how some folks might mistaken them as either a bit withdrawn or maybe even mean, but she assured him that they are really a nice bunch of folks.

"Thanks for the warning, and it was a pleasure chatting with you" Jack said as he headed off.

Jack jumped backed into Johnny B and headed down Fillmore Historic Main Street where he arrived at Cluff's Car Hop Café. It was a cool little retro spot that offered outside patio seating under a corrugated tin-metal carport awning and umbrella covered tables on the left side of the patio. The front of the building was constructed with red, pink, black and grey bricks with old school hubcaps hanging over the front door. Old school 50s diner décor hung on the walls inside the cafe. Empty vintage soda bottles of various brands and sizes sat upon a shelf that lined one side of the walls as old Utah license plates hung along the perimeter on the other side. The menu offered a conglomeration of your typical 50s dinner food items like hamburgers, hotdogs, specialty sandwiches, milk shakes and malts.

Jack stood behind a family of four who were placing their order. The man of the family was writing down their order on an order pad. Jack thought that it must have been a big order, but then realized what was actually going on when the man began to use sign language to communicate to his wife. It was then that Jack realized that the man was deaf. The man's wife asked each of their kids what they wanted to eat as she signed back to her husband who was writing the order down.

After the man completed his order, Jack stepped up to the counter and ordered a grilled cheese sandwich and chocolate malt. Jack thought to himself, "A good old fashion grilled cheese sandwich sounds pretty good right now." Just as Liz warned him, the workers were a bit peculiar in their own odd way.

Jack sat outside under the tin-corrugated carport awning while the family that was in front of him in line sat a couple of tables over. The family appeared to not have much based on what they were wearing. Their clothes were fairly tattered and the kids' shoes were practically falling apart. But one thing was evident to Jack;

they appeared to be a very happy family. The husband showed subtle signs of affection towards his wife, and the kids were both courteous and very well behaved. Jack stared, as he was fascinated at how the family communicated with one another with sign language even though he himself couldn't understand.

One of the gals from behind the counter brought out Jack's sandwich and malt. Jack couldn't help but continued to observe the signing between the family members. He wondered what their conversation was all about. Jack mustered the courage to engage in conversation with them.

"Hello," Jack said, "I couldn't help but admire how young your kids are and am impressed by how well they are able to use sign language."

The wife replied, "Oh, thank you. They've been learning ever since they were born."

"How old are they," Jack asked.

"Leslie is five and Jake is three."

"They are also very courteous and well behaved," Jack added.

"Thank you. I'm not sure if I can take credit for that or not," the wife said shyly.

"By the way, my name is Jack."

"My name is Emily and this is my husband Nathan." Nathan waved at Jack.

As Jack nodded back to Nathan he asked, "Do you guys live out here in Fillmore?"

Nathan signed to his wife and Emily relayed back to Jack, "No, we happen to just be stopping by on our way back home to Cedar City."

"Oh," Jack replied, "I was just there this morning. I had breakfast at this quaint little coffeehouse called the Grind Coffeehouse."

"We know and love the place," signed Nathan.

"How about you? Where are you headed?" signed Nathan as Emily translated.

"I'm headed up I-15 towards Canada."

"From where?" Nathan signed.

"San Diego."

"Do you have family in Canada?" asked Nathan.

"No. I just decided to hit the road and head northward to clear my head."

"Must be a lot of 'clearing' that needs to be done. Canada is quite a drive from San Diego," Nathan signed with a huge grin.

"Yeah," Jack giggled. "Where are you guys coming from?"

"Salt Lake City," Nathan signed, "I had a job interview up there."

"What was the job?" Jack asked shyly.

"It's a construction job. They seemed really interested in my resume and wanted to interview me, but I obviously couldn't do it over the phone, so we made arrangements to drive up there."

"How did it go if you don't mind me asking?"

"I don't mind at all. I think it went well. Either way, I'm pretty happy where I'm at now. If they hire me in Salt Lake City, it'll be a definite raise in salary. Regardless of how it turns out, I'm pretty content where I am now," replied Nathan.

As both Jack and Nathan's family enjoyed their meals, their conversation went from casual to deep in a matter of minutes. Nathan began to open up about how he used to be resentful at life because he was born deaf. Being deaf was a huge challenge let alone just trying to get through life. Nathan explained how he used to focus on all the negatives in his life. His dad was fed up with having to raise a deaf child that he left him and his mother. Nathan was about five years old at the time. His mom suffered an early stroke and was challenged to raise Nathan all by herself. Nathan explained how they lived in poverty for most of his teenage life. He struggled academically throughout school. Nathan's mom died of a heart attack when graduated high school. He went to live with his uncle in Arizona who got him into construction. That's where he met Emily who was waitressing at a bar at the time. They got married and immediately started their family. They lost their first child to SIDS at four months. Jack didn't notice, but Leslie is blind in one eye and Jake is autistic. Life has been really hard on Nathan.

Emily stopped signing and told Jack that despite all the challenges in life that Nathan has faced, he is the happiest and most thankful person she has ever known. "Life has taught him how to be content, and he has learned to appreciate what has been given to him both good and bad," Emily said with a smile.

Nathan signed to Emily, which she translated back to Jack. "He wanted you to know that he also can read lips and wanted you to know that he knows what I just told you."

Jack looked Nathan straight in the eyes and said, "You're a rare breed Nathan. Whether you know it or not, you have found the key to happiness in life."

"What is that?" Nathan signed as Emily continued to translate their conversation.

"Contentment," Jack answered. "There's an ancient and sacred book that says, 'Godliness with contentment is great gain.'"

"You're referring to the Bible right?" Nathan signed.

"Yes," Jack responded surprised.

"I'm very familiar with it," as Nathan replied signing.

So Jack shared with Nathan a passage out of the Book of Philippians regarding what the apostle Paul wrote regarding contentment. He said that he knew how to be content whether he had a lot or whether he had a little. He also knew that he had Christ who would provide everything that he would ever need in life. Jack went on to explain how people are never satisfied. They are constantly complaining about their situation and life. They either want more money, nicer cars, bigger homes, better relationships, higher degrees, greater promotions, more of this or more of that. Those who are fat want to be skinny, and those who are skinny want to gain weight. Those who are short want to be tall, and those who are tall want to be shorter. The list goes on and on. No one is happy. No one is satisfied. No one is content.

The secret to a happy life is appreciating everything we have instead of complaining about what we don't have.[7] It truly is about counting our blessings every day. Contentment is what we should strive for. "And you my friend have discovered that secret," assured Jack.

"I'm not a religious man Jack, but I've learned early how to appreciate all that the Good Lord has blessed me with. I know that life is not fair. I understand that bad things happen to good people and vice versa. In all of it, I have also learned not to be resentful, angry, bitter, or play the victim," explained Nathan. "Growing up with very little has caused me to appreciate everything. Like Emily said earlier, I've learned to appreciate and accept both the good and the bad. I believe all things happen for a reason. I just try to take life one day at a time and not take for granted the blessings I get to have and experience everyday."

Jack thought of an old story he once shared with his congregation about a poor old man who sat alone on Christmas Day ready to eat a crusty old piece of bread for dinner, for it was all he had. As he bowed his head in prayer to give thanks, his simple words said it all as he eyed his small piece of bread, "All this and Jesus too!" The old man realized that despite his lack of material things, he had an abundance of spiritual things in Christ. He had God's love, God's grace, God's forgiveness, God's blessing, God's provision, and God's gift to him of eternal life. He understood how spiritual things were much more valuable than material things.

Nathan and his family finished their meal, gathered their trash, and began to head towards their car.

Jack got up, shook Nathan's hand, and bid him farewell. "Thank you for taking the time to chat. And thank you for reminding me of the wonderful and humble lesson on contentment. I am glad to have had the privilege and honor to meet you and your lovely family. God bless you Nathan."

"And God bless you too Jack," Nathan signed in return.

Sitting back down to finish his grilled cheese sandwich and chocolate malt, Jack thought, "All this and Jesus too!" as he smiled contented.

Trust in the LORD with all of your heart and lean not on your own understanding.

Proverbs 3:5

CHAPTER 8
The Breakdown

As Jack approached Salt Lake City, he noticed that the steering on Johnny B abruptly became rather difficult. The alignment felt off, as there was a slight pull towards the right as he steered. Concerned, Jack immediately pulled off of the interstate and into a gas station with a garage.

He walked up to the service counter and rang the bell. A gentleman in blue overalls with a white oval nametag with the name "Floyd" embroidered on it came up to the counter and asked Jack, "How can I help you?"

"I own the Chevy Fleetwood Jamboree out front. The steering seems off. I think it might be the alignment. It just started pulling to the right making it difficult to steer. I managed to get off of the interstate safely to pull into the station," Jack explained.

Floyd handed Jack a clipboard and asked him to fill out the upper half with his information on it. Then he asked Jack to pull his RV in as close as possible next to the garage entrance.

Floyd examined Johnny B and came back to give Jack his assessment. "At first I thought either you were low on power steering fluid or the power steering belt was either lose or damaged," Floyd said initially. "Unfortunately, your power steering pump is broken. But let me check real quick; I think I might have one in inventory."

Floyd checked the inventory on his computer. "The computer says I have one in stock, but let me double check the back just to make sure I have it." Floyd disappeared into the back stockroom and in a couple of minutes returned with the part in his hand. "You're in luck. I did have it. It should take me a couple of hours to install if you want me to do the work."

"Yes please," Jack replied. So Floyd wrote up a quote for Jack to sign and then started to change out the pump on Johnny B.

Jack headed over to the gas station right next to the garage, which had a convenience store in it. In the warm food case you can find deep fried food items like French fries, fried chicken, corndogs, and burritos. It was your typical convenience store with snacks on the shelves, drinks in the coolers, and even souvenirs of various kinds on racks. On one rack hung wooden slingshots and Daniel Boone style frontiersman hats that were covered in fake fur with raccoon tails attached to the back of them.

As Jack looked around, his eyes widened as if he had just spotted gold! Gas station beef jerky! Jack loved gas station beef jerky. They are the the kind that are not packaged but sold individually in Plexiglass stands with the little metal tongs attached to the stand by a plastic coiled bungee cord. Karen always questioned how sanitary it was to sell or serve food snacks in such a manner; she was somewhat of a germophobe. Regardless, Jack couldn't resist. His favorite was the hot and spicy ones that Karen couldn't handle. She rarely would indulge in spicy foods.

Stepping outside, Jack sat on the bench next to the big white refrigerator that stored bags of ice for sale. He leaned back enjoying his gas station beef jerky. He looked like he had a wad of chewing tobacco in his mouth. As Jack sat there, a glare from the ground below caught his unprotected eyes. The glare was blinding for less than a second, but it was intense enough to grab Jack's full attention. As Jack adjusted his head position and looked down, he noticed that it was a brand new shiny penny on the ground that caught the sun's rays at the most precise angle. Jack picked it up and recited the words of Proverbs 3:5, "Trust God will all of your heart and lean not on your own understanding." It was a habit Jack had established years ago. His perspective changed after he read an article online where the author talked about how he viewed random coins on the ground as subtle reminders from God to trust in Him. The author of the article mentioned how all U.S. coins have the phrase "In God We Trust" inscribed on each of them. Since then, Jack never missed the opportunity to pick up any coins on the ground that he came across. He'd recite the verse from Proverbs 3:5, put the coin in his pocket, and then placed them in a coin jar when he got home. On the coin jar, Jack put a label with the Proverbs 3:5 verse printed out on it.

The first few months that Jack established the habit of picking up coins and reciting the Proverbs 3:5 verse, he coincidentally found himself in situations where he desperately needed to trust in God. The funny thing was that throughout those first few months, Jack started to realize that when he came across coins of a larger denomination, like dimes or quarters, he found himself in more challenging situations. The higher the currency's denomination was coincidentally indicative to the magnitude of the challenge he would eventually have to face. At one point, he was afraid to pick up any more coins knowing that challenges awaited him in the near future that would require a greater trust in God. One time he came across a twenty-dollar bill and purposefully told a random stranger that he dropped some money just to avoid having to pick it up himself. Jack was trying to avoid any uncomfortable life-altering challenge. There was one time when he went for a casual run around his neighborhood and came across a penny on the street. As he tried to pick it up, he realized that it was permanently embedded into the asphalt. From that experience, Jack concluded that God was trying to tell him that he needed to always trust in Him.

For Jack, trusting God daily was simply about obeying God. God desires us to obey the instructions He provides us in the Bible. Little do we realize that those instructions are for our own good. When a person obeys God and learns to put their trust in Him, they step through the threshold of faith and into a realm that is filled with God's wonderful blessings and provisions. The entirety of the Christian faith is about trusting God. Trusting God is not part of Christianity, it is Christianity. Trusting God opens doors to wonderful opportunities in the Christian life. Trusting God allows for Christians to express their faith in active and practical ways that open the door for God to work wonderful things in their lives.

Jack understood that trusting God is like a train of dominoes falling. Trusting God is obeying Him; obeying Him is loving Him; loving Him is knowing Him and His love for us. The more and more you read the words of the Bible, the more and more you'll know God and His love for you. God reveals Himself through the words of the Bible. And as you get to know God, you'll see yourself in light of His truth. The more you learn to know God and His love for you, you will find yourself compelled to love Him in return. And loving Him is expressed by obeying Him. And obeying Him is neither a burden nor a responsibility but rather an opportunity for our faith to grow and to witness God's amazing work unfold in our lives. When you obey Him, you demonstrate how much you trust Him. Trusting God stems from knowing God. And when you trust Him, the door of faith opens up an abundance of His blessings upon your life.

What was this penny for? Why the reminder to trust God? What challenge was he about to face? Was it about Hannah? Or Jimmy? Was it for Johnny B? Was it for something this road trip has in store for him? What does God has in store for him? Regardless, Jack knew that he needed to simply trust God. He knew from experience that trusting God took all that he had. But when he did trust God, he would experience a peace that was incomprehensible. It was a peace he couldn't explain. It was a peace he knew that God had his back. It was a peace that he knew God would work everything out for Jack's own good. It was a peace that everything is going to be ok.

Jack learned that when life appeared to be "breaking down" per say that it was the time he really needed to trust God. It was during times when things were not going his way. It was the times when things were not working out. It was the times in Jack's life when things were uncertain. Even when things looked hopeless, it was then that Jack learned that he really needed to put his faith and trust in God. And God can be trusted. God knows everything from the beginning to the end. Too often we do not realize that God is neither restrained nor restricted by the boundary of the dimension of time that we as humans live in here on earth. We think that we know our situation better than anyone else. We think we know what's best for us. But God knows better than us. God knows exactly what we need and when we need it. There are things that are far beyond our understanding that only God can understand. God is also sovereign and has complete control over of all things. Even when our world is spinning out of control, God is still in control working all things out for each of our benefit. Trusting God allows God the opportunity to work in our lives and predicaments in a way that He is only able to do. He knows what He is doing. Though we may not understand it, God's way are not like our ways. His ways are far better than ours. His methods are far more efficient than ours. His answers and solutions make a far greater impact in our lives than our own. And God has our very best interest in mind simply because He loves and cares for us like no other. He is a good, loving and compassionate God. And He can be trusted.

In the Book of Psalm 31, King David penned these words during a time when he ran for his life from his predecessor King Saul who was determined to kill him. Amidst the ordeal, David resolved to trust in God. Here are some of the words David uses in this particular Psalm:

shame, trap, affliction, anguish, distress, weak, sorrow, grief, groaning, fails, contempt, dread, and *terror*. These words describe some of our most desperate times. The words of Jesus Christ as He died on the cross for all humankind was quoted from this Psalm. David and Jesus knew that they had a Heavenly Father who they could trust their lives to. Trusting God unleashes the work and power of God's mighty hand in our lives for our benefit and for His honor and glory. Trusting God allows for God's good plan to work itself in and through our lives. Trusting God opens the door to wonderful and amazing outcomes. Our greatest blessing lies on the other side of trusting God.[8]

Jack stared at the shiny penny for a second as he focused on the words "In God We Trust" that were inscribed above President Lincoln's head. Karen had always been Jack's safety and comfort. Whenever Jack had a rough day, he would come home and just nestle himself into Karen's arms and place his head in the nape of her neck. When he caught a whiff of her hair, he found an incredible release of all the day's stresses and pressures. It was what he did to calm himself during tough and stressful times. Jack couldn't stand getting immunizations. He hated needles. Whenever he would have to give blood at the doctor's office, he would have Karen there next to him so that he could hold her hand and smelled her hair. Her touch and her scent was a stress reliever for Jack. It was how he kept calm during stressful situations and circumstances. But now she was gone. Jack no longer had Karen to hold his hand. He no longer had Karen's hair to smell. As all the thoughts of Karen raced back through his mind, he found his heart wrestling with feelings of grief, doubt, and fear. How would life be without Karen? What will he do when he comes home from a tough day? Where will he lay his head to find comfort? Whose hand will he hold the next time he has to give a blood sample? Whose hair will he smell to calm his anxious heart? He was at a point of breaking down. But oftentimes, that's where God meets us. Oftentimes God meets us at our breaking point. In our weakest and most vulnerable moments, we can rest assured that God is there extending His hand for us to hold and His arms for us to collapse in.

All of a sudden Jack was overwhelmed by a barrage of thoughts and memories of Karen. It flooded his heart. It flashed through his mind like a movie on fast forward. He could see Karen's face. He remembered the warmth of her touch, the sound of her voice, the smell of her hair, and the taste of her kiss. He was overwhelmed with emotions of love, joy, and excitement that were muddied with sorrow, grief, and sadness. He missed her. He missed her dearly. He longed for her. He longed to have those moments again. It ached in the deepest parts of his bones. But then he realized that there would be no more of those experiences with her. Now they were just memories. He couldn't fathom the thought. He couldn't grasp his current reality. He couldn't imagine his future without her. He could no longer contain himself. He clasped his face into his hands as his eyes flooded with tears and ran down his face as he wept uncontrollably. He broke down. All the memories and feelings culminated into one thought for Jack in the form of a question. How was he going to live without her? How was he going to get through this? Jack has lived through some tough times before, but losing Karen was the worse. He felt as if though the walls of his heart were closing in on him. The pressure inside was building up and the pain and hurt was simply unbearable. Who would he turn to? Who could he trust? The very One that could be trusted sat right next to him on that bench outside that gas station. He had always been there, and He will always be. God has never left him nor will He ever forsake him. Especially in his brokenness.

Jack had trusted God many times, and he was certain that he could trust God again. He knew his life without Karen would not be easy, but he couldn't image a life without God. A God who he could trust. A God who loves him like no one else. A God who will never leave him nor forsake him. In that moment, Jack wiped away his tears, bowed his head, closed his eyes, and struggled to utter this prayer from his heart:

Dear God,
I know you love me like no other, and I know that I can trust you with my life. I cannot see tomorrow like you can, and I do not know how things will work out in the end. But I know You do. So help me to trust in You. Help me when I doubt. Strengthen my faith. Even in these desperate times I know that You have my back. You have always been faithful, so whatever I may face, help me to trust in You. In Jesus' name. Amen.

Just as Jack uttered the final words of his prayer, a peace so overwhelming came upon him that calmed his mind and thoughts and brought healing to his aching heart. It was a supernatural peace beyond all understanding that he had experienced many times when he turned his eyes toward God to trust Him. Jack's brokenness was an entry point for God to come in and bring healing and reassurance. God can only fix what is broken.

A few minutes later, Floyd came walking up to Jack wiping his hands with a towel.

"Well, I got her all fixed up for you."

"It's a 'he,'" Jack whispered to himself. "Thank you so much Floyd."

"I just need to finish the paperwork so that we can get you back on the road."

Jack got off the bench. And as he made his way back towards the garage, he happened to spot a quarter on the ground in front of him. He shook his head, looked up towards heaven and smiled.

"For my thoughts are not your thoughts, neither are your ways my ways," declares the LORD.

Isaiah 55:8

CHAPTER 9
The PK

With Johnny B all fixed and ready to go, Jack made his way back onto the interstate. Just shy of reaching Idaho Falls, he pulled into a Love's Travel Stop to hunker down for the evening. Love's is a family-owned chain of truck stop and convenience stores located throughout the United States. The facilities offer travelers a place for food, gasoline, convenience store items, restrooms and showers 24-hours a day. Jack stopped at one that had a McDonalds restaurant attached to it. "Driving stirs up quite an appetite," he thought. Jack was ready to satisfy his Big Mac attack.

After ordering his meal, Jack decided to sit next to the window. While staring out into the parking lot at his RV, he noticed a young girl get out of the passenger side of a car that was driven by a young man who immediately sped off as she shut the door. Her red eyes and running mascara made it obvious that she had been crying. Trying to wipe the smudged makeup from her eyes, she walked inside of the McDonalds and hesitatingly placed her order. She took a seat in a booth that faced Jack. Trying hard not to stare, Jack couldn't help but wonder how old she was. She looked fairly young. Jack grew concerned whether she was a victim of some sort.

Taking his tray to the trashcan as he was about to head back to his RV, Jack decided to stop to talk to the young lady. "Are you ok? It looks like you have had a rough night. I couldn't help but notice that you have been crying," said Jack.

"Yeah, I'm good," she replied.

Jack stood there for a few seconds as he did not quite believe her and asked, "Are you sure?"

She was small and fragile but determined to show that she was strong and capable of taking care of herself. As Jack continued to stand there, she broke out in tears. Concerned, Jack grabbed some napkins and came back asking, "Do you mind if I just sit with you for a little while?"

"Sure. I don't mind," she responded as she wiped the tears from her eyes. So Jack took a seat directly across from her.

"My name is Jack."

"I'm Peyton."

"Well Payton, it's a pleasure to meet you."

Jack sat there quietly for a moment to allow Peyton the time to decide how much she wanted to tell him. After all he was a complete stranger.

"So there's this guy," Peyton started as she gripped the ends of her long sleeve flannel shirt. "He took off on me."

"I'm assuming you're referring to the young man who dropped you off earlier?"

"Yeah," replied Peyton. "I told him I was pregnant," as she looked down in embarrassment.

"Let me guess," Jack interjected, "He asked if the baby was his?" Jack said rhetorically.

"Yeah, how did you know?" Peyton asked as she slowly looked up in surprise.

"I've been around the block a couple of times now sweetie, so there's a few things that I know about life."

"Well," Peyton continued. "I told him it was his because I hadn't been with anyone else. Then he told me that I should get an abortion, and I told him 'no'. I told him I was going to have the baby with our without him."

"Well good for you," said Jack.

"Well..." Peyton started with great hesitation, "...to be honest with you, I've had abortions in the past, but for some reason this time it's different. I really want to have this baby," explained Peyton. "Vernon said he wasn't ready for it. He threatened to leave the freaking country if I had the baby just to avoid the whole fatherhood situation. Can you believe him?"

"I'm assuming Vernon is that guy we're talking about?"

"Oh, yeah, sorry."

"No worries. Just want to make sure I know who we're talking about."

"So that's when he dropped me off here."

"Just out of curiosity, why here?" Jack asked.

"Because we were on our way here to get some fries and that's when I decided to drop the news on him," Peyton replied.

"Oh I see. So what are you going to do now?" Jack asked with concern in his voice.

"I don't know."

"Where's your family?" asked Jack.

"Oh, there up in Idaho Falls," replied Peyton, "But, I'm a little scared and ashamed to tell them."

"I don't know your parents, or the full extent of your story, but I'm sure they love and care about you and will understand."

"Yeah, you don't know my parents. For starters, my dad's a pastor."

"Really?" replied Jack surprised to hear that her dad was a pastor. "What does that mean?" wondering what she meant by her dad being a pastor.

"It means he's going to be really pissed off and disappointed that I got myself into this situation. I can see his face now," as she shook her head knowing how upset and disappointed her dad would be.

"I'm assuming you haven't spoken to them about any of this."

"Nope," Peyton responded.

"I personally believe that there's this huge divide between kids and their parents that prevent them from really having a really good and close relationship," explained Jack. "I understand some of the dynamics that are involved, but I think that kids and parents can be so much closer if they both try to understand each other a little more."

"Yeah, I guess so."

"So you think your parents won't understand?" asked Jack.

"I think they expect a lot from me that I'm unable to live up to," Peyton sadly replied. "Like when I graduated from high school, I got married to my boyfriend. My parents weren't too happy about the idea. They thought I was really young and immature. But they respected the fact that I was an adult and could make my own decisions. A couple of years later, we got divorced, and I know that killed my dad. He really liked the guy too."

"So what are you going to do?" Jack probed.

"I really don't know."

"Why don't you try talking to them?" asked Jack trying to encourage her.

"I wouldn't even know what to say or where to begin. In the past I've lied to them just so that they don't get upset or disappointed in me."

"Do you think that's best?"

"No. But I just can't stand how my dad is when he gives me this look of silence. And then to top it off, he gives me the cold shoulder treatment where he doesn't say anything. He does this passive aggressive thing that I can't stand. It drives me nuts."

"Why not just try being honest with your folks?"

"I don't know," replied Peyton. "I don't think I can live with their disappointment. I'd prefer that they just didn't know some of the things I do or even some things about me. I think they'd die if they found out."

"Are you able to open up to me because I'm a complete stranger?" asked Jack.

"Maybe," replied Peyton, "I don't know what it is, but I actually feel really comfortable telling you stuff. You seem really kind. And I feel like you won't judge me either. And you seem like a good listener."

"I've had a lot of practice," Jack said jokingly. "Do you think your parents listen to you?"

"I believe they do, but I think they could do better trying to understand me. It takes more than just listening."

"I hear you," Jack reassured her.

"I think my dad doesn't agree with a lot of my life's choices," explained Peyton. "I feel like I have to behave a certain way. I feel like he wants me to be someone I'm not. That's why I feel like he really doesn't understand me."

"Maybe he's just being a parent," offered Jack.

"What do you mean?" asked Peyton.

"Parents want the best for their kids, and it hurts them to see their kids hurt. They want to see their kids be happy and lead successful lives. They just want the best for them, but it can come across wrong. The message gets lost in translation," explained Jack.

"You sound like you speak from experience."

"You're right. I have a daughter myself. She's all grown up and doing well now, but admits that she's made some pretty bad decisions in the past and even confessed how she probably should have listen to me and taken my advice on a few things."

"I know that there's a reason for the way things turn out, and I know that God will work it all out," said Peyton.

"So do you believe in God?" Jack somewhat asked.

"Definitely. I'm what they call a 'PK,'" explained Peyton.

"I'm familiar with the acronym," Jack interjected.

"I grew up in church," continued Peyton. "I know all the Bible stories. My dad tries his best to encourage me in my faith. Sometimes he's subtle at it and other times he's pretty overly direct. Sometimes I think he thinks I've given up on my faith."

"Have you?" Jack asked out of curiosity.

"Well, for one thing, I don't go to church. But I still read my Bible and pray once in a while. I don't know if my prayers really make a difference anymore. Sometimes I think God stopped answering my prayers because of all the bad stuff I've done."

"I hear you, but oftentimes I have discovered that God's ways are not necessarily our ways. In other words, I find that God answers our prayers but not in the way we would like for Him to. You said that you know all the stories in the Bible right? Do you remember the one about Naaman?" asked Jack.

"No. You'll have to refresh my memory about that one," replied Peyton.

"In the Book of 2 Kings 5, a man by the name of Naaman, who was a commander of the Syrian Army had leprosy. He went to seek after God for his healing from the prophet Elisha. Elisha instructed him to wash in the Jordan River."

"Oh yeah, I remember now," Peyton interrupted. "He was the guy that didn't want to wash in the Jordan River because there were better and cleaner rivers to wash in right?"

"Exactly," said Jack. "Namaan questioned the manner and place to wash. He knew that the Jordan River was a very dirty and muddy river not suitable for drinking or even washing clothes. He wondered why he wasn't sent either to the rivers of Damascus like the Abana or the Pharpar. But eventually Naaman did what Elisha instructed him to do and dipped himself seven times in the Jordan River, and God healed him of his leprosy."

"Good thing he did what Elisha told him," said Peyton.

"Could you imagine if Naaman had dismissed the instructions Elisha gave him? Imagine if Naaman had decided to listen and went to the Jordan but only dipped six times. Do you think he would have received his healing?" asked Jack.

"I don't know. Probably not?" replied Peyton unsure.

Jack explained to Peyton that God has this incredibly good and wonderful plan for each of our lives, and He amazingly works in and through the details of everything that happens to us in order for His good and wonderful plan to work itself out. In the end, we are able to look back and be amazed at how God used those things, both good and bad, to make us better for it. At the time, we just don't understand why things happen the way they do, but we should trust that God is working it all out for our own good. In the Book of Isaiah 55:8, it tells us that God's thoughts and ways are not like ours simply because they are better. Way better! We should be careful to never question the manner or method by which God will act nor presume how He should answer our prayers; otherwise, we can miss out on His wonderful blessings for our lives.[9]

"You sound like my dad when he preaches," Peyton remarked.

"Is that good thing?" chuckled Jack.

"Yes it is," Peyton assured him. "My dad's a really good preacher. He's a good pastor too. And a good father."

"That's encouraging to hear you say Peyton. Then I think you can talk this over with him, and I'm certain he and your mom will be there for you."

"Yeah, you're probably right."

"Plus," Jack added, "They're going to be grandparents. That is definitely something good and wonderful to celebrate!"

"I hope so."

"Stay right here. I'll be back," Jack told her.

Jack ran next door into the convenience store and bought a little stuffed teddy bear and a bag of diapers. He handed them to Peyton and said, "You're going to need a lot of these."

Touched by his gesture, Peyton came over and gave him a hug and said, "Thank you."

"You're welcome," Jack said. "Can I give you ride somewhere?"

"No, I'm good Jack. I got a text from Vernon saying that he's coming back to pick me up."

"Are you going to be ok?"

"Yeah, for sure. Now that I got to meet and talk to you."

"Take care of yourself Peyton and the lil' one you're carrying. And do me a favor."

"What's that?" asked Peyton.

"Take it easy on your folks. Trust me. They really do love and care about you."

"I know," smiled Peyton.

As Jack walked out into the parking lot towards his RV to retire for the evening, Peyton watched him leave as he looked back at her. As he got into his RV, he waved bye to Peyton and closed the door behind him as she smiled and waved back.

For we do not have a high priest who is unable to empathize with our weaknesses, but we have one who has been tempted in every way, just as we are - yet he did not sin.

Hebrews 4:15

CHAPTER 10
Just Wanting To Be Understood

The following morning Jack headed up towards Idaho Falls. He was preoccupied with thoughts of Peyton on the drive up. She had reminded him so much of his daughter Hannah. She was strong-willed yet so fragile. Jack hoped that his talk with her last night had encouraged her to talk with her parents. He prayed for her as he drove. Praying was a way that helped Jack release his cares and concerns about people and situations to God. It was a way to release heavy burdens that weighed heavily on he heart.

Immediately upon arriving in Idaho Falls, Jack stopped for breakfast. He searched for a local joint on Yelp and found Smitty's Pancake & Steak House.

Immediately upon entering the restaurant's foyer, Jack noticed that the window facing the street was adorned with a myriad of different colored chalice glasses that lined several shelf inserts. Gold colored old school style lamps hung from the ceiling everywhere. Fine china adorned the shelf that lined the perimeter wall with two huge gold colored plates engraved with a design that Jack could barely make out. It looked like it was either Jesus teaching his disciples or an old lady weaving a rug while her family members surrounded her. An old brown coffee bean grinder with a gold colored pot attached to it sat on a small table next to the cash register booth. Gold frame paintings adorned the walls. A gold color ceiling fan with wood-stained colored fan panels hung over the cash register booth. Practically everything in Smitty's was dark brown in color, the windowsills, carpet, tables, chairs, wall panels, and even the cut out letters behind the cash register booth that spelled out "Welcome." Gold and dark brown were the décor colors that provided a warm, cozy, and welcoming atmosphere.

A sweet charming gal seated Jack in a booth next to a window that faced the street.

"Can I get you something to drink?" asked the server.

"Coffee and a glass of water please," replied Jack. "What's your name?" he asked the server. Again, it was Jack's habit to ask and address his servers by their names. He always felt it was more personal.

She smiled and said, "My name is Katherine," and then headed back to the kitchen.

Another young gal came by and reached over Jack's table adjusting the window blinds in order to shade the sun's rays from shining into the eyes of some customers seated at the table next to Jack's. "Pardon my reach," she politely told Jack.

As he waited for his coffee, Jack noticed a photograph of an elderly couple standing in front of a tour bus that was hanging on the wall near him. When Katherine returned with his coffee, Jack asked her whether it was a picture of the owners.

"Yes it is," Katherine responded. "The current manager is actually their granddaughter. So what can I get you?" she asked pulling out her notepad ready to take Jack's order.

"I'll have the pancakes please."

"Side of bacon or sausage?"

"I'll have the bacon."

"Ok, I'll have that right up."

Jack noticed the gal who lowered the blinds earlier and asked her, "May I speak to the manager please?"

"I'm the manager," she replied. "How can I help you?"

"Katherine told me that you are the granddaughter of the original owners?" inquired Jack.

"Yes, that's true. My name is Katrina."

"Hello Katrina, my name is Jack. When my wife and I travel, we make it a point to eat at local establishments that are unique to the area. Basically, we try out places that we can't get at home."

"Where's home?" asked Katrina.

"San Diego."

"And where's the wife?"

"She's no longer with me. She recently passed away."

"Oh, I'm so sorry to hear," responded Katrina sympathetically.

"Thank you," replied Jack. "Most local establishments have interesting stories behind them. Any chance this one does?"

"As a matter of fact, this restaurant used to be a part of a franchise," Katrina informed him. "Until my grandparents Leo and Cleo Werner bought the restaurant back in 1971."

"Is that right?" Jack asked surprisingly.

"I took my first job here when I was 14 years old filling condiments."

"Now look at you," Jack interjected, "You're running the place!"

"I really love working here," Katrina said proudly. "It makes me really proud to be a part of something that my grandparents worked so hard for."

"Well, thank you for sharing that story Katrina."

"It was my pleasure," Katrina smiled.

Jack sat and enjoyed the most delicious stack of pancakes he had ever eaten. As he sat there, he couldn't help but overhear the conversation between a young girl and her father in the booth directly behind him.

The young girl appeared to be in her early twenties, and she was trying to convince her father that she wanted to move to Southern California to make a life out there for herself. The father was pleading with his daughter not to go. He reasoned how it would be a bad idea for her to leave Idaho for a pipe dream. Jack thought that his concerns were pretty legitimate, but what the dad failed to do was really listen to his daughter. Not just listen, but also listen empathetically with the intent to understand. Jack was quickly reminded of his conversation last night with Peyton and how she desperately wanted to be understood.

"Dad, you don't get it. Why can't you please understand?" asked the young girl in desperation.

We all want to be understood. Jack equated understanding people as a form of grace. Grace is one of the many gifts of God. Grace is unmerited favor. Grace is receiving God's love, kindness, compassion, mercy, and blessings even though we don't deserve it. Grace gives us room to discover ourselves in light of God's goodness. Grace allows for us to appreciate God's goodness despite what we discover about ourselves. But grace is also putting ourselves in other people's shoes and trying to understand them.

When people understand one another, they allow each other room for both error and differences. It gives them the opportunity not only to express themselves but also to learn and grow as people. Understanding people allows for grace to be extended towards others in a way that fosters an environment of love, care, respect, and acceptance. Understanding comes from putting yourself in another person's shoes. Seeing through their eyes, their contexts, their viewpoints, and their perspectives. Feeling their hurts, pains, and frustrations. It's about empathy.

That is exactly what God did when He sent His only Son Jesus in the form of humanity and then demonstrated His love for each of us when He voluntarily gave His life on the cross for the forgiveness of our sins. And when we believe in Him, we have been graced by God's incredibly wonderful gift of forgiveness leading to eternal life.

Jack felt both empathy and sympathy for this young daughter as he did for Peyton. They were two young girls just wanting so desperately to be understood. We all want to be understood. All too often we find ourselves in predicaments when we feel like we are all alone. Circumstances where we feel like nobody understands, where nobody knows what we are going through. In our moments of fear, doubt, shame, embarrassment, guilt, or loneliness, we feel like no one understands what it's like to be in our shoes. But that is not the case when it comes to God. God know and understands. God is so full of grace.

Jack was reminded of the story in the Book of Mark 4:35-40 when Jesus was in a boat with His disciples as they were in the midst of a raging storm. Jesus was asleep in the boat when His disciples woke him up afraid for their lives. They were afraid that the storm would capsize their boat causing them all to drown. They asked Jesus if He cared that they were in the midst of the raging storm that had the violent potential to kill them all. Did He care? That's what they asked Jesus. Did He care? When Jack first read that passage in the Bible, one of the most insightful details he noticed was that Jesus was in the same boat as His disciples. Jesus was in the same boat, amidst the same violent storm, facing the same life-threatening situation. The passage taught Jack how Jesus is always in the same boat that we find ourselves in. When we feel like no one knows or understands what we are going through or the challenges we face, we can rest assured that Jesus does.

Another Bible passage from the Book of Hebrews 4:15 explains how God Himself became human in Christ to demonstrate to us how He has affiliated with our humanly and earthly sufferings, challenges, and temptations. God is not out of touch with our reality but completely understands us.[10] God has put Himself in the same boat as we are in to demonstrate to us how much He understands and cares about us. Jesus can still calm the storms in our lives today the same way He did in that boat over two thousand years ago. Jesus truly understands every aspect of our situations, and

He is there to reassure us that He loves and cares for us.

"I don't understand why you feel the need to move so far away from home," said the father. "I'm just not sure about this sweetie. We don't even know anyone in Southern California."

As Jack continued to listen in, he contemplated whether this was an opportunity to say something. Was this an opportunity to help this young girl live out her dream while giving her father some peace of mind? Jack couldn't pass up the opportunity, so he leaned over to catch the eyes of the father and said, "Hi, my name is Jack. I did not mean to eavesdrop, but I couldn't help but overhear your conversation. I'm a retired pastor, and I just came from Southern California. I'm a father of a daughter myself, and I can completely understand where you're coming from. I personally know a pastor and some wonderful people from the church I just retired from that would love to help in any way make your daughter's dream to move to Southern California come true. Our church has actually helped others transition to San Diego. They have helped people find a place to stay. Other members of the church have actually taken in complete strangers in order to give them a place to stay until they can find a place of their own. They have even help people find jobs. "

As the daughter turned around to hear Jack's offer, a glimmer of hope could be seen in her eyes as she turned back to her father for a response.

"Thank you for your kind offer," the father replied. "I guess it couldn't hurt to check it out."

Jack had an old business card from his wallet that he took out and handed to the father.

"By the way, my name is Larry and this is my daughter Trisha. She just graduated high school last year and has been dreaming of California for a very long time now."

"I understand kids want to spread their wings and venture out of the nest, so I get it. I also understand as a father my concern and over-protective instincts for my daughter, so I get that as well. So the number on the card is actually no longer number but now my good friend's office number who took over as the pastor when I retired. Just tell them Jack sent you. His name is Terry, and his wife's name is Abby. I've done ministry together with them for decades. They're really good people with really big hearts to serve," reassured Jack.

"Thank you," replied Larry. "I really appreciate the offer."

Trisha looked at her dad with excitement.

"I'll talk it over with your mom, and we'll see," as Larry tried to calm her down.

Larry took a final gulp of his coffee and got up with Trisha. As they were leaving, Larry waved Jack's card and said, "Thanks again."

"My pleasure," responded Jack.

As Jack finished up his pancakes and coffee, he felt a sense of pride to have spoken about his church the way he did. He had the wonderful honor and privilege for over three decades to serve as the pastor there. He knew that the church was a loving and grace-filled community that acts more like an extended family. He knew the people of his church and how they love serving others. He hopes that Larry will call and discover that the people of his church are genuine, good-hearted, and want to help. As Jack remembered back on the years that he served as pastor there, the one thing he thinks of automatically is the people. They were not just his congregants; they were his friends and family. Jack hopes that Larry will give them an opportunity to show that to Trisha, and that he can trust that she will be in good hands.

But the Lord answered and said to her, "Martha, Martha, you are worried and bothered about so many things; but only one thing is necessary, for Mary has chosen the good part, which shall not be taken away from her."

Luke 10:41-42

CHAPTER 11
Time Well Spent

Montana was definitely one of the most beautiful states that Jack has ever visited and driven through. He was completely enamored by the blanket of trees that covered the surrounding the mountain ranges. The subtle lakes and rivers that ran through the forests added a touch of serenity to the scenery. Driving through was one of the most peaceful and calming moments Jack had ever experienced. The amazing vastness of the sky looked as if it came straight out of a painting and justified why Montana was known as Big Sky Country.

Jack detoured into the city of Helena. As he drove through the city streets, one of the first things he noticed was that practically every other establishment appeared to have the word "casino" in its name. He had never seen more casinos in one place other than Las Vegas.

According to a Google search that he did, the "casino" establishments in Helena applied for a license to only have slot machines on their premises. Despite the word "casino" in their name, there is no legalized gambling, per say, in Montana.

Jack stopped in downtown Helena for a bite to eat. As he walked down Last Chance Gulch in the downtown area, Jack came across a corner café named Murry's. It was a chic kind of place that appeared to be expanding. As Jack walked up to the counter to order, he noticed the lunch specials written on a dry-erase board that hung above the counter. The menu comprised of healthy American and ethnic cuisine items. Today they offered an array of Thai curries. Jack ordered the Thai green curry with chicken over basmati rice.

Jack took a seat at a table in the front dining area of the restaurant. As he waited for his order, he noticed artwork that hung on the walls. On one side hung canvases of what appeared to be sepia tone photos that highlighted the architecture of old buildings. On another wall were photographs from a wildlife photographer that were actually for sale. On another wall hung local awards and reviews on the restaurant. There was also a framed article from a local newspaper that tells the story of the owners and how the restaurant was started. The article displayed a picture of what appeared to be an older-looking guy and a young girl who started the place.

As an artist himself, Jack admired the canvased prints and wonder if they were photos of actual buildings from the downtown area. So he approached a young lady behind the counter and asked, "Are these canvas photographs of downtown Helena?"

"Why yes they are," the young lady replied. "Actually, they are my pieces."

"Oh wow," exclaimed Jack. "I'm a photographer myself. I happen to have my undergraduate degree in art. I actually had my first photography exhibit in a small café in San Diego just a few months ago. My name is Jack, and I just put two and two together and noticed your face from the article hanging on the wall back there. Are you one of the owners?"

"Yup, that's me," replied the young gal, "I'm Joanie."

Joanie took off her apron, laid it behind the counter, and came around to explain to Jack each of her photographs. She was very friendly and hospitable. Knowing that Jack was from out of town, she pulled out a printed map of downtown Helena, and showed Jack where the restaurant was located and where he could actually find each of the buildings in her photographs if he so desire to.

Jack couldn't help but ask, "So what exactly is 'Last Chance Gulch'?" Is it a downtown district of some sorts?"

Joanie explained to him that it is the actual name of the street that the restaurant was on. She also explained to him that the name has a unique and interesting history. She shared how Helena was actually an old mining town back in the old western pioneering days. The story goes that four men from Georgia came out to Western Montana to mine for gold but found none. They stumbled into this place we now know as Helena. On the evening of July 14, 1864, they decided to take one "last chance" to mine for gold, and little would you know, to their surprise, they struck gold.

"They named the stream that they found the gold in 'Last Chance Gulch,' and that's how the name came about," explained Joanie.

"No kidding?" Jack said surprised.

"That's the story," Joanie assured him.

"Wow, that's pretty cool!" smiled Jack. "Thanks for sharing Joanie."

"My pleasure," Joanie said as she returned the smile.

Jack sat back down at his table and inhaled his meal. He was so hungry, and it was absolutely one of the most delicious Thai curry dishes he had ever had. As he was finishing up on the last few bites, he noticed a middle-age businessman dressed in a suit. His jacket and attaché case hung on the back of his chair. His tie was flung over his shoulder as to avoid any stains as he hurriedly tried to finish his lunch while on his cellphone. Jack could barely make out his conversation, but it sounded like he was on the phone with his wife explaining why he couldn't be back in time for his daughter's soccer game. As he reached over to type something on his tablet, he knocked over his drink spilling it on the notepad on the table in front of him. Liquid ran everywhere and quickly soaked through some of the pages of his notepad and then onto the floor. Jack immediately went to grab a handful of napkins to help him clean it up.

"Oh, thank you," the man said to Jack.

Jack began wiping up the floor with the napkins when Joanie came out with a bucket and mop to clean up the spill.

"You look like you're one busy guy. Are you trying to close a big deal before the lunch hour ends?" Jack said jokingly.

"No, I'm just trying to finish the notes of a sermon that I'm going to preach," replied the man.

"Oh, so you're a pastor?" Jack asked surprised.

"Yeah, I pastor a church in Southern California, but I'm the keynote speaker for a conference that's being held here this weekend. I've just been so busy with a lot of things."

"You do look a little like you're moving at warp speed," said Jack. Jack noticed how the pastor looked extremely stressed and tense trying hurriedly to dry off his notes. "Feels like there's no time to slow down huh?"

"Exactly," responded the pastor.

"But you know that's when you should consider slowing down right?" Jack asked wryly.

The pastor suddenly stopped all he was doing, closed his eyes, took a deep breath, mouthed a couple of words as if he were saying a prayer, opened his eyes, looked Jack straight in the eyes while putting his hand on Jack's forearm and slowly said to him, "You're completely right. Hi, my name is Rick," said the pastor.

"It's a pleasure to meet you Rick. I'm Jack. I used to be a pastor too."

"A brother who can relate," Rick said with a sigh of relief. "Please feel free to join me if you'd like."

"I wouldn't be interrupting? I'd hate to take you away from your busy schedule," responded Jack.

"You'll be more of a much needed break from all of this. Trust me, you're probably an answer to my prayers," Rick said as he pulled out the chair next to him inviting Jack to sit down with him.

"Well, ok then," replied Jack as he accepted the invitation and sat down. "What's the conference about?"

"It's a leadership conference for local church pastors," replied Rick.

Rick explained how he was invited to be the keynote speaker by a denomination of churches in the area, and he couldn't refuse.

"I have a Ph.D. in church leadership," Jack shared.

"Where did you get your Ph.D.?" asked Rick.

"Regent University in Virginia Beach."

"I've heard of their program," responded Rick. "I know of a couple of pastors and friends who've done their doctoral work in that same program. Interested in a job?" Rick asked jokingly.

"Oh no, I'm retired," replied Jack.

"I feel like I'm ready to do just that," said Rick.

The next several minutes Rick shared with Jack how he's been tirelessly and relentlessly doing ministry for the past 15 years and how he's been feeling burned out. He also shared some of his honest feelings of resentment. He openly shared with Jack some of the difficult people he not only had to deal with in ministry but those who he personally felt have turned against him. He explained how, as a pastor, he had invested so much time, energy, and emotions into caring for people who have shown no appreciation but have later been the source of criticism, gossip, and slander. "You think they're your friends and you treat them as such…" expressed Rick, "…but in the end they leave your church and talk bad about you to the rest of your congregation. You not only feel unappreciated for the things you've done for them but also betrayed having left you hurt and resentful."

Jack began to share with Rick how a few years ago he was in a similar place in his life and ministry. He realized later that he had been seeking the approval of people rather than the approval of God. As humans, it is natural for us to want to be liked, affirmed, and appreciated. We should be careful when we start to expect these things from the people we minister to. Because when we don't receive these things, we can oftentimes find ourselves hurt and resentful.

Jack also explained how easy it is to allow the work of ministry to become the distraction itself. He personally shared how he was burned out by ministry too. He was so busy doing ministry and ministering to others that he neglected ministry to himself and to his family. He had allowed the work of ministry to become an idol in his life that took away from his personal devotion time with God. Through the experience, God taught Jack that his ministry would be a direct reflection of his own personal relationship with God. In other words, if his relationship with God was good, then ministry would be good. But if his relationship with God was not so good, then ministry would reflect that as well.

Jack reminded Rick of the story in the Bible about Mary and Martha. They were sisters who hosted Jesus and His disciples in their home. Martha was busy and distracted with all the preparations, while her sister Mary sat at the feet of Jesus and spent time listening to Him as he taught. Frustrated, Martha asked Jesus to tell Mary to help her. Jesus told Martha that she is worried and upset about many things, but only one thing is necessary and Mary has made that choice. The choice Mary made was to sit at the feet of Jesus and listen to and spend time with Him. One thing is needful. The most important thing we can do that will profoundly impact our life and the life of others is wholly contingent upon the time we spend with Jesus.[11] We can be so busy with work, family, hobbies, and other things that we fail to do the one thing that is truly necessary and so desperately needed. That one thing is to spend time with God. Even the apostle Paul explained in Philippians 3:13-14 that the "one thing" that was important to him was to pursue after Christ. In 1 Corinthians 9:27, the apostle Paul also expressed how he didn't want to be hypocritical in the way he lived his life of faith. During his time, he preached to the people, but wanted to ensure he was living what he was preaching.

Jack asked Rick, "In making disciples for Christ, have we stopped being disciples ourselves? In other words, how far have we've grown apart from God in trying to help people get closer to God?

Jack's words deeply convicted Rick to the core. "I know all this," said Rick.

"What we know does not necessarily mean it's what we practice," Jack replied as a subtle admonishment.

"How deep are you going to dig that knife in my back Jack?" Rick said jokingly.

"As deep as it'll take to surgically remove the very things that keep you from seeing the truth and living the blessed life that God has in store for you," Jack replied with a caring grin.

"From one pastor to another, I really appreciate that," Rick said with a serious tone, as he looked Jack straight in the eyes.

"I hear the hurt and frustration in your words Rick. I know the place that all of this is coming from because I've been there before. I just want to encourage you to focus on God's love for you and how you can love Him in return."

Rick glanced at his watch and realized how late it got. "Well, I got to get going," said Rick. "I appreciate your time and words of wisdom and encouragement Jack. Could I ask you to pray for me?" Rick humbly requested.

"I would be most delighted and honored to," replied Jack.

Jack placed his hand on Rick's shoulder as they both bowed their heads and closed their eyes in prayer.

When Jack finished praying, Rick took out his business card and handed it to Jack saying, "Seriously, if you want a job, I sure could use your help."

Jack smiled, thanked Rick for the offer, and replied, "You have all the help you need."

Rick smiled back, threw his trash away, gathered his belongings, and rushed out the door.

As Rick left, Jack wondered whether Rick was truly going to slow his pace in ministry and life. As a former pastor, Jack could empathize with what Rick was dealing with. Too often ministers can be so engrossed in their ministries that they fail to see how their personal lives are swinging out of balance. Jack had first hand experience of this in the past, but he learned to ensure he established healthy spiritual rhythms like Bible reading, prayer, worship, and fellowship in his life that kept him balanced.

Taste and see that the LORD is good...

Psalm 34:8

CHAPTER 12
Probability

After lunch, Jacked decided to take a stroll down Last Chance Gulch in downtown Helena. The weather was perfect for a stroll. The shops and cafes that lined both sides of the street were welcoming and enticing. Just a few shops down from Murry's, Jack came across the Fire Tower Coffee House. He couldn't deny his caffeine craving.

Like many other distinctively unique coffee shops, Fire Tower was unique in its own right. Cozy sofas and armchairs bookended a variety of tables that were scattered throughout the café. In the front corner of the coffee house stood an old school jukebox and at the other end an imitation fireplace. The kitchen was closed off by a half-wall that started from the hardwood floor. Several stuffed burlap sacks printed with various coffee bean vendors from places like

Mexico, Columbia, Brazil, Ethiopia, and Costa Rica hung from the wall. Canvased photographs of The Beatles from a local artist also hung on the wall. Inside the coffee house above the entrance was a nostalgic toy fire truck.

The server was an older gentleman in his late forties who kept his bleached white hair cut extreme short just shy of his scalp. Jack couldn't tell if his hair was naturally white or dyed. His black-framed glasses made him look nerdy yet quite fashionable. He wore an unbuttoned white and blue flower print shirt over a red t-shirt that had a white peace symbol print in the center. He wore blue jeans that were held up by the most outrageously cool white belt with images of The Beatles all around it. Jack thought for sure he was most likely the owner but didn't bother to ask.

Jack ordered a house coffee. The server rang up his order and handed him a plastic frame with the picture of R2-D2 from the Star Wars movie that served as a place stand. The server told Jack to place it on his table, and they'll bring out his order.

Jack found an open table against the wall. Right above his table hung a wall ornament made out of carved wood that read "TRUTH." Jack couldn't help but stare at the carving while he pondered on what could have provoked the designer to select such a word.

"Everything controversial packed into one single word," remarked a stranger that sat at the table next to Jack's. He couldn't help but to comment on Jack's moment of reflection.

"Why do you say that?" asked Jack.

"Well, truth is relative right?" the stranger asked back.

"Not necessarily. One of the first things that came to my mind was an ancient character in Jewish/Roman history from an Old Book I've read who asked the question, 'What is truth?'" Jack shared.

"Oh yeah, what book is that?" asked the stranger.

"The Good Book," replied Jack with a wryly grin.

"You must be referring to the Bible," said the stranger.

"So you're familiar with it?" asked Jack.

"Who isn't?" retorted the stranger. "It's supposedly the best-selling book of all time according to the Guinness Book of World Records."

"I've heard that, but you'd be surprised at how many people aren't familiar with it," replied

Jack. "Do you happen to know the story in the Bible that I'm referring to?"

"You're referring to the story about when the Roman Governor Pontus Pilate asked Jesus what the meaning of truth is right?"

"Yes, exactly," replied Jack.

"And you're going to tell me that Jesus is the truth right?" the stranger asked cynically as he slightly rolled his eyes.

"I personally believe He is," replied Jack. "Jesus even said that He is the Way, the Truth, and the Life." Jack probed the stranger by asking, "What is it that you believe?"

"I'll tell you what I don't believe," retorted the stranger. "I don't believe in God for one. It's hard for me to believe in God. I personally feel that no one can really prove that God exists."

At that moment, a server brought out Jack's coffee. He placed the cup on Jack's table and was about to take away the R2-D2 place stand when Jack asked if he could hold on to it for a second. The server obliged and returned back behind the counter.

"Are you familiar with R2-D2?" Jack asked as he showed the place stand to the stranger.

"Who isn't?" replied the stranger.

"I recently read something interesting online that explained how Star Wars creator George Lucas attributed the origins of 'The Force' in his Star Wars movie series from a 1963 abstract film by Arthur Lipsett. Lipsett took the concept of the force from a conversation he heard regarding how people are aware of some kind of phenomenon that they attribute to that links people and creation. It so happened that the phenomenon they referred to was God."

   Jack continued, "George Lucas admits this is where he draws from his idea of the force. Remember the famous words of Obi-wan Kenobi as he explains the force to Luke Skywalker in the original movie? 'The force is what gives a Jedi his powers. It is an energy field created by all living things. It surrounds us, penetrates us, it binds the galaxy together.' Don't you think there is something true about a phenomenon that surrounds us, penetrates us, and binds us together?" asked Jack. "A phenomenon that is the source of our life and why we exist?"

   "It's possible, but how is that related to what we know as truth?" asked the stranger. "I believe that truth lies beyond merely one religion or from the teachings of one man. I don't understand how one religion can be right and every other religion wrong. What are the chances that Christianity is right? What are the chances that it's wrong?"

"Good question," replied Jack. "I may not have the answer, but I can tell you what I know and what I have experienced."

"And what's that?" asked the stranger.

Jack began to briefly share with him his spiritual journey and how he personally came to an understanding of who Jesus is and why Jack believed in Him.

The stranger found Jack's story and experience quite intriguing but still questioned, "How can you be sure you're right?"

"My faith makes me certain," replied Jack.

"But it's a blind faith," retorted the stranger.

"Not necessarily."

"From my understanding from reading and studying the Bible and talking with other Christians is that you all claim that Jesus is God. How can you all be so certain?" asked the stranger.

"So how in depth have you 'studied' the Bible?" asked Jack.

"I grew up as a Christian. My parents were Christian. We went to church every

Sunday. But when I became an adult, I decided to do my own thing," the stranger explained.

"Have you read the passages in the Bible that assert that Jesus is the Jewish Messiah? That He was the predicted Savior of the world?" asked Jack.

"I know that there are these so called 'prophecies' that predicted that Jesus is this Jewish Messiah, but what are the chances?"

"It's interesting you ask," replied Jack. "Have you heard about an actual study that was conducted by a university professor that practically proves beyond a reasonable doubt that Jesus is the predicted Jewish Messiah?"

"No."

"Would you like to hear it?"

"Sure. I like to consider myself pretty open minded," the stranger smirked as if to imply Christians aren't.

Jacked preceded to share with the stranger how a university professor conducted a study with 12 different classes that comprised of 600 university students on the probability that Jesus could have fulfilled eight biblical prophecies that referred to His Messiah-ship. Jack explained to the stranger that the chances for Jesus to fulfill only eight specific biblical prophecies regarding the Jewish Messiah was one in 100 quadrillion. In order to put that number in perspective, Jack explained that the probability of becoming The President of the United States is one in 10,000,000. Jack further illustrated to the stranger the actual probability of Jesus fulfilling only eight of the 300 biblical prophecies regarding the Jewish Messiah. He explained that the probability would be like covering the entire state of Texas with silver dollars perfectly stacked two feet high, one on top of another, and marked only one of them, and then try to successfully pick out that one marked silver dollar while blindfolded. "Those odds are amazingly slim," remarked Jack. "It's easier to win the lottery than for that kind of odds to take place."

"And I assume Jesus did this?" asked the stranger. "He fulfilled these eight biblical prophecies that you speak of?"

"No," replied Jack. "He actually fulfilled over 300 biblical prophecies regarding the Jewish Messiah. Now imagine those odds!"

Jack shared with the stranger the startling conclusion that the university professor made. He asserted that anyone who rejects Jesus as the Messiah is rejecting a fact proven by statistics. Even other mathematicians and statisticians who are not Christians have acknowledged that it is scientifically impossible to deny that Jesus is the Jewish Messiah. Jesus is truly the Son of God. The probability that Jesus Christ is truly the Son of God is undeniable, but no one can convince you unless you give God the chance to prove Himself to you personally.[12]

Jack went on to share a couple of other reasons why he personally believes that Jesus is who He says He is. Jack explained how Jesus predicted His death and His resurrection from the grave. How can anyone do that? He also shared the historical accounts of Jesus' appearance following his death by not only his close followers but by 500 others as further evidence. Jack also explained the unrelenting faith of His close followers that further demonstrated what they each truly believed in. He also explained how Jesus' disciples were cowards who feared for their lives the moment Jesus was arrested and crucified but then risked and even gave up their lives to proclaim the Good News of His resurrection. Jack asked the stranger why would they risk all and give up their lives if they knew that Jesus' resurrection was a hoax and not true? Jack explained how today that there are over two billion Christians, and the Christian church continues to grow. But the most profound reason that Jack believes in God is because of the billions of lives that have been transformed by this truth. The destitute have found hope; those bound in addiction have found freedom; those afflicted have discovered healing; those broken are restored; those lost have found their way; those discarded have been redeemed. And the most significant of those lives was Jack's.

"You're argument is fairly compelling," commented the stranger.

"It's not an argument. It's simply what I believe that has been substantiated by my own real and personal experiences," replied Jack. "And you know what they say about a person with an experience."

"What's that?" asked the stranger.

"A person with an experience is never at the mercy of a person with an argument," replied Jack. "I'm not here to convince you to believe all that I have shared with you. It was simply my intention to engage in conversation with you and share what I know and what I've personally experienced. I enjoy engaging complete strangers in conversation about Jesus. Oftentimes I learn from it myself."

"What have you learned from ours?" the stranger asked.

"I've learned that it doesn't matter how hard you try to convince someone that God is real, you can't make them believe. You get the wonderful opportunity to meet people God loves and cares about and add to the conversation that God has been having with them all along. And that's good enough for me."

"You think God has been having a conversation with me?" the stranger asked Jack.

"Definitely. And I just got to jump into it for a little while."

"Interesting perspective."

"One thing I didn't learn that I would like to is your name," Jack added.

"It's Irvin."

"I'm Jack. It was a pleasure to make your acquaintance Irvin. Thank you for the dialog," as he extended his hand out to Irvin.

Irvin shook his hand and replied, "It was nice meeting you too Jack."

As Jack grabbed what was left of his coffee and preceded towards the door, he looked back and said to Irvin, "Don't give up on God. He hasn't given up on you. Give Him a chance. Chances are, He won't disappoint you."

"I'll keep that in mind," said Irvin as he nodded his head as a courtesy and lifted up his cup of coffee to Jack.

The mind governed by the flesh is death, but the mind governed by the Spirit is life and peace.

Romans 8:6

CHAPTER 13
The Governator

The clean crisp morning air filled the cabin of the RV like a fog settling upon a calm lake before dusk. Jack wore a Regent University hoodie from his old alma mater. He loved hoodies. It was his favorite article of clothing. He describes it as a sleeping bag that you can wear. It kept him warm enough so that he could keep the windows to the RV open to enjoy the smell of the fresh morning air. Jack continued to enjoy the drive through Big Sky Country. He took his time driving through Montana as he admired the vastness of the land as it was lit up by the sunlight bursting through the cloud-covered skies. The scenery reminded him a little bit of the western side of Colorado. He and Karen drove through there on their way to Quantico where Jack attended the Marine Corps' Basic School as a newly commissioned officer.

The few times Jack and Karen drove across country, they would take the southern route on Interstate 10; however, they decided to take the northern route on Interstate 70 wanting to explore new and unfamiliar territory.

Jack pulled into Great Falls and stopped at the Loaf 'N Jug gas station to fill up Johnny B's tank and to empty his tank. Afterwards, he stopped by to Ford's Drive-In next door for a quick bite to eat.

Jack noticed the 8'6" vehicle clearance sign that hung just slightly below the drive-in carport at Ford's and decided to park Johnny B on a side street next to the drive-in. As Jack took a gander at the menu that hung overhead, a young girl in jeans and a t-shirt darted out of the drive-in restaurant towards him and asked, "What can I get you?" From the looks of the place, Jack was kind of expecting her to be wearing a poodle skirt and roller skates while holding a serving tray and smacking on some chewing gum.

"What's good?" asked Jack as he continued to look over the menu.

"Everything," replied the young girl.

"Then I'll have the cheeseburger, an order of French fries, and a chocolate milk shake please."

Jack always loved a good cheeseburger. A cheeseburger and French fries was Jack's definition of comfort food. He always made it a point when traveling to find the best burger joints in town to eat at. He's been to some of the country's famous burger joints like Gordon Ramsey's BurGR, Bobby's Burger Palace, Holsteins Shakes and Buns, Wahlburgers in Las Vegas, and San Diego's famous Hodad's. He even enjoys some of the well-known franchises like Red Robin, Burger Lounge, Krystal, Shake Shack, White Castle, Five Guys, Smashburger and The Counter. But his all time "go to" burger joint is In-N-Out. Once in a while Jack would treat himself to a chocolate milkshake with his cheeseburger. He oftentimes never drank it with his meal but would save it until the end as dessert.

"I'll have that right up for you," smiled the young girl.

Jack grabbed a seat on one of the wooden picnic tables under the shade nearby. As he sat there waiting for his order, he noticed several vehicles parked under the carport where everyone else was eating their meals in their cars. Jack felt that he was missing out on the full drive-in experience.

As Jack sat enjoying his cheeseburger, he noticed the odd bright color of the drive-in building. The color was similar to a Tiffany-blue. It was the colloquial term used to describe the trademark blue of the bags used by the New York City jewelry company popular known as Tiffany. Instantly, it reminded Jack of the many pieces of jewelry that he had bought Karen on their anniversaries. Jack and Karen mutually agreed that Jack would only buy Karen jewelry on their anniversary. All of Karen's jewelry that she wore or owned was anniversary gifts from Jack throughout the years. Not all of them came from Tiffany's but a good portion of them did.

All of a sudden a deep and familiar sadness fell over Jack once again. It was a weighty presence that overrode every moment of his current reality. Thoughts of Karen once again began to invade his mind. The thoughts were all pleasant thoughts that were now juxtaposed with a deep and clawing sadness of loss and grief. Jack desperately tried to fend them off. He struggled whether to suppress his feelings or simply embrace them. They were thoughts of Karen. Pleasant thoughts of her would gradually transitioned into reminders that she was gone.

All it took was a simple trigger. In this case, it was the Tiffany-blue color of the drive-in building. From it coalesced a barrage of images that unleashed a satchel of uncontrollable emotions. It felt as if the scab on a wound had been plucked once again, and blood began to ooze fresh. It was a wound that was not going to be able to ever heal properly. It would become a wound that would leave a scar. Thoughts of Karen flashed through Jack's head. Feelings of love and lost coupled with fear and uncertainty emerged once again. How was he supposed to deal with this? When would it eventually end? Did he even want it to end? If it did, would that mean he was over Karen? Did he want to be over her? A myriad of thoughts flowed one after another as it began to cloud his mind as the heaviness pressed upon his heart. Jack felt as if though his heart was going to explode.

Studies have shown that a person processes an average of 60,000 thoughts per day. That comes down to about one thought every one and a half seconds. Studies have also revealed that 94 percent of those thoughts are in regards to a person's needs, wants, and concerns. Jack was reminded of how negative thoughts can easily send a person into a downward spiral. It can send them into an extremely slippery slope into some dark and evil places. Jack remembered a time when he was working to complete his doctoral studies. A comprehensive exam was required after a student completed all of their academic coursework. It was an exam that was only allowed to be taken twice. Two failed exams would result in the student not being allowed to start the work and research on their dissertation, which would mean that they wouldn't be able to graduate and receive their degree.

The first time Jack took his comprehensive exams, he failed. It was one of the most devastating moments of his entire life. Now Jack was under immense pressure to pass the exam for the second time. It plagued him with negative thoughts and doubts. What if he didn't pass? All those years of work completing the coursework, all that money spent on tuition, books, fees, and associated travel expenses to the campus for residencies during the program would all go to waste. This led Jack into a downward spiral of stress, anxiety, depression and even physical illness. Jack remembered a cognitive neuroscientist that asserted how 75 to 80 percent of physical illness can actually originate from a person's thought life. What a person thought could actually have an effect on their physical health.

During this time, Jack was reminded of the Scripture verse in Romans 8:6 that tells us that a mind that is governed by the flesh leads to death, but a mind that is governed by the spirit leads to life and peace. The act of governing is to control, restrain influence over or keep in check by right of authority. Governing one's thoughts is controlling what one thinks about. It's restraining influence over the things we think about. It's keeping in check negative thoughts. This is accomplished through the power and authority given to us by Christ. We govern our thoughts by controlling them, restraining influence over, or keeping in check through the power of the Holy Spirit. With an average of 60,000 thoughts per day, it's easy to be bombarded by negative thoughts. Those negative thoughts could be of past guilt or present failure, worries and concerns, or fears and uncertainties. There exists a constant tension between the thoughts that we think. It's like a war that rages in our minds. In the Book of Romans 7:22-23 it explains how there is a force that is at work that wages war against our minds and holds us as prisoners. This never ending conflict in our minds between the negative things we think of and the positive and faith-filled thoughts of God's Spirit rages within each of us. It is tempting in the midst of bleak and disparaging times to think negatively. In these vulnerable moments of our lives, it is extremely tempting to give into fear and doubt. But if we believe and trust in the empowering of God's Spirit to help us think on the good thoughts that God wants for us to think on that lead to faith, then we can experience a life of peace and joy. If we think negative, then our outlook becomes negative which results in despair. But if we think positive, then our outlook becomes positive which results in hope.

Jack was reminded that walking victoriously in the power of God's Spirit could be accomplished by making the deliberate choice to govern his thoughts. God makes it possible for us to rule over negative thoughts by allowing God's truth that is reveal to us in the Holy Scriptures not only to fill our thoughts but also to prevail as reality in our lives. The apostle Paul wrote in the Book of 2 Corinthians 10:5 that we have the power in God's Spirit to demolish arguments and every pretension that is contrary to the knowledge and truth that God has revealed to us in the Bible. We allow our thoughts to be governed by what the Bible says about who we are, what we have, and what were are capable of doing and accomplishing in Christ. In the Book of Philippians 4:8, the apostle Paul instructs us to think on things that are true, noble, right, pure, lovely, admirable, excellent, and worthy of praise. The writer of the Book of Hebrews 3:1 says to fix our thoughts on Jesus. Jesus is the paradigm of all things good and perfect; therefore, allow His goodness and attributes to be the focus of our thoughts. In order to have a happy and healthy life, you have to make a choice to begin by ridding yourself of toxic thoughts and begin to think on happy and healthy things that are in alignment with what God thinks of us. The Bible is filled with the thoughts of God towards us. We are undeniably shaped by the thoughts we think; therefore, allow our thoughts to be shaped by what God thinks of us.[13]

Jack learned to govern his thoughts during this challenging time of his life. There were times when those negative thoughts, fears and doubts would creep back in, but he continued to exercise gaining control over his thoughts and align them with the authority of what is revealed to him in the Holy Scriptures. Jack remembered how he would live by the power of the Holy Spirit to govern his thoughts and having faith in God.

Jack also remembered the moment he discovered that he had failed his first comprehensive exam. In the midst of his disappointment, he balled up into a fetal position in bed and cried his heart out. He remembers Karen comforting him and praying for him. He clearly remembers her exact words to him. She told him as she rubbed his back, "Jack, I know this news is really disappointing and not what you were expecting. Get your one good cry in, let it all out, then pull up your bootstraps and get back in. You got this. This is only a temporary setback." And that is exactly what Jack did.

After taking his second and final chance at his comprehensive exam, Jack kept his thoughts fixed on Jesus. He allowed his mind to be ruled by the truth found in God's Word. By doing so, he knew that regardless of the results of his exam, he knew who he was, what he had, and what he was capable of doing and accomplishing in Christ. The results of the exam would not change any of that. He knew that by overcoming the negative thoughts, doubts, and fears and remaining centered on the positive thoughts that are outlined in the Bible, it would allowed him to live in a supernatural peace that only God could provide.

Jack eventually passed his exam. The moment he received his results, Karen asked him whether he felt any difference between the time he felt before he knew he passed and now knowing that he had passed. He told Karen that he really didn't feel any different. He admits that he's definitely thankful and relieved that he passed, but there was no real difference in his attitude because he allowed his mind to be governed by the Spirit of God. In other words, Jack maintained having good and positive thoughts that were more a reflection of his faith in God. He knew God loved and cared for him. He knew he could trust God. He knew God was in control. He knew God had his best interest at heart. He knew God had a plan for him that was good. Because all these things are revealed to him in the Bible. Those were the thoughts of faith that governed his mind, and so he was at peace through it all.

The day when his exam results came out, Jack's sister-in-law text messaged him and asked him how he did. He told her that he passed. She responded, "Glad it was victorious in the end!" He text messaged her back, "It would have been victorious either way, but I know what you meant." He added a little smiley face emoticon at the end of the text message to her. Jack knew he was victorious in Christ despite whether things went his way or not.

Jack could not deny how deafening the Tiffany-blue color of the drive-in building initially was. It screamed out memories of his anniversary celebrations with Karen. He allowed his thoughts to get away from him resulting in a barrage of overwhelming emotions. But with the help of the Holy Spirit, Jack has the power to govern those thoughts into ones that were more indicative of his faith and trust in God. He allowed the thoughts to be ones that were lovely, excellent, and worthy of praise. He allowed the thoughts to reaffirm God's love for him, God's sovereignty, God's omniscience, and God's good plan for the remainder of his earthly life. Jack allowed those good thoughts to engage his faith that would suppress any worry, anxiety, doubt or fear. Jack allowed the Tiffany-blue color to be one of celebration rather than one of grief. It represented gifts of celebration of his and Karen's love and commitment to one another. In that moment, Jack felt an indescribable peace. It was a peace that reassured him things were going to be ok. That he was going to be ok.

But our citizenship is in heaven.

Philippians 3:20

CHAPTER 14
Into Another Country

It was as if it was the end of the road. Upon reaching Sweet Grass on the edge of the U.S. border, Jack debated whether to cross over into Alberta, Canada or just turn around and head southbound back to San Diego. He pulled over into a duty free shop and fill up his gas tank while mulling over the decision. He figured he'd gone this far, so why not cross the border? He'd never been to Canada before. So Jack decided that he would pop in and then pop right back out of Canada just to say he'd been there.

As he pulled up into the Canadian border services agency, the agent stationed in the booth asked for Jack's passport and then started to barrage him with a myriad of questions. What is the purpose of your trip? Where will you be staying? Do you happen to be carrying large sums of cash on you? Have you been convicted of a crime in the U.S.? Jack felt like he was being interrogated as a suspect of a crime. But after a round of satisfactory responses, Jack was allowed entry into the country of Canada.

As he made his way into the tiny town of Coutts, he pulled over next to a small brown building that had a sign on it that read "Market Place." Flags of Canada and Alberta hung in front of the building, and the town's name of "COUTTS" was spelled out in bricks and stones on the ground. Jack parked Johnny B next to the building and then took a seat at a picnic table nearby. Sitting in silence, he thought to himself, "Wow! I'm in another country." It wasn't his first time in a foreign country. He had visited the Philippines as a child. During his time in the Marine Corps, he did a tour of duty in Korea and Japan. He took Karen to Cabo San Lucas for their honeymoon, and they also went to the Bahamas for their 13th anniversary. He's been on countless mission trips to Mexico and even visited some missionary friends of his in Thailand. But for some inexplicable reason this time, just meters from the U.S. border, it felt different. For some reason, Jack had a greater sense of awareness of not being a citizen in a foreign land. Maybe it was all the questioning by the border services agent. Who knows, but for whatever reasons, it was different this time.

Immediately Jack thought of what the apostle Paul referred to in the Book of Philippians 3:20 when he wrote that as believers in Christ, we are citizens of heaven. That this earth is not our home. Jesus explained in His prayer found in the gospel of John 17:15 that we are not of this world. Though Jesus has sent us into the world to share the message of hope in Christ, we were created for another world. A far better world. Our life here on earth is only temporal; yet as we live it, we should have more of an eternal perspective. The way we live our lives should reflect our faith to live the rest of eternity in a place beyond this one. The way we treat others, spend our time and money, pursue our dreams, as well as the way we play, share, and love should all be reflected in our faith. Every aspect of our lives here on earth should be viewed through the perspective of where our souls will live for all eternity. The writer of the Book of Hebrews 11:13 speaks of Old Testament characters of faith who lived their lives as foreigners and strangers here on earth. In Hebrews 11:16 it tells us that they looked forward to a better country. They looked forward to a heavenly country. A country that was difficult to describe because mere words could not capture the essence or magnitude of its beauty. Deep down in the aching of our souls is a longing for a better world than the one we currently live in. It's something out of this world. Jesus said in the gospel of John 14:2 that there is a place in heaven that God has prepared for those who believe in Him and who have put the faith and trust in Christ. God has placed a longing in each of us to seek after Him. It is a longing inherent in each of us that nothing but God can satisfy. People have tried to satiate this longing with money, material things, fame, relationships, sex, drugs, and everything else imaginable; but nothing other than God can quench this thirst and hunger. Saint Augustine called God "the end of our desires" and prayed, "you have made us for yourself, O Lord, and our hearts are restless until they rest in you." British novelist and Christian apologist C.S. Lewis said, "If we find ourselves with a desire that nothing in this world can satisfy, the most probable explanation is that we were made for another world." Each of us has been created to live with God in a world far beyond the one we currently live in. Our hearts ache deeply for it. For some, it's apparent; but for others, it'll take a myriad of events and circumstances to transpire before they come to a realization of the truth of it.

At that very moment, Jack looked up into the sky and was captivated by how the sunbeams majestically broke through the cumulous cloud cover. It reminded him of a time in his life when he was driving home from work one day. On that particular day while driving onto the exit towards home, Jack caught a brief glimpse of the sky. It was the same majestic scene that captivated him now. Jack experienced a brief moment of an inexplicable feeling in his soul. The only way that he could describe the feeling was like being homesick. But it wasn't being homesick for his earthly residence, which was only a few blocks away, but rather a homesickness for this heavenly abode. It was a tension between his temporal and earthly life and his eternal and heavenly destiny. It must have been the feeling that the apostle Paul describes in the Book of 2 Corinthians 5:8 when he explained how he would rather be with the Lord than here on earth. At that very brief moment driving down that off-ramp after work, all Jack could think about was heaven. He was captivated by a longing in his heart for where he truly belonged. It was the place where he was reborn in Christ and now claimed citizenship. It was his place of origin, and his heart was now well aware of it. It was a place we refer to as heaven.

Now sitting on that picnic table in the foreign land of Canada, Jack recalled the words of the apostle Paul in the Book of Colossians 3:2 to set our minds on things above and not on earthly things. We become so engrossed in the things that are temporal in our lives, such as material things that quickly vanish. We fail to set our thoughts on more heavenly and eternal things. Looking through the lens of eternity allows the thoughts we have of heaven to have an amazingly eclipsing effect that puts all things earthly and temporal into proper perspective.[14] Once again, Jack found himself overwhelmed with that feeling of homesickness for heaven. Maybe it was the sunlit clouds in the sky. Maybe it was being a foreigner in a foreign land. Or maybe it was because he missed Karen so much and longed to be where she was. For whatever reason, he longed for a better place and a better country. A place described in the Bible where there will be no more tears and no more pain. A place where the water is as clear as crystal and the streets are as shiny as gold. A place where there are angels. A place where the Lord will be. And a place where Karen is waiting for him.

Jack had been on the road for quite some time now. Johnny B had been his temporary home, and now he sensed a longing to get back home to San Diego. It was an exciting journey for Jack. He had longed to live off of the road in an RV. The thought of experiencing new and unique places beyond the horizon were tantalizing. The thought of having a new front yard everyday was enviable. The feeling of freedom to go wherever your heart and curiosity would take you is adventuresome. But home will always call you back, and Jack sensed that it was time to head back. It's exciting to be in a foreign place, but sooner or later you'll long for home. So Jack got back into Johnny B and headed back into the U.S.

The U.S. border patrol agent was much more interrogative than was the Canadian one. After going through a barrage of similar questions at the border patrol booth, Jack was asked to pull his RV into the parking lot at the station and enter the building. After checking in with the border patrol agent, Jack was asked to remain in the lobby while they thoroughly searched his vehicle. As he sat there, he saw two agents go through his vehicle inside and out with a canine that was probably sniffing for controlled substances.

After what felt like an eternity, Jack was cleared to enter back into the U.S. Once Jack got his passport back from the border patrol agent, he jumped back into Johnny B and headed out of Sweet Grass southbound onto Interstate 15.

Jack was baffled by how much sunlight was still out late that evening. At that time of the day, the setting sun created magnificently warm and amazing colors against the sky. As Jack made his way southbound towards Great Falls, he noticed that there was nobody else on the road. The interstate was completely empty. There was no vehicle traffic either north or southbound on the interstate for as far as Jack could see. All he could see were just the distant mountain ranges on his left, the clouds and sky above, the sun to his right, and the road beneath him. At that very moment, Jack felt as if though he was the only person on the face of the earth. It was like when God created Adam in the beginning. For Jack, it felt like it was just him and God. It was a secluded yet surreal moment for him.

All of a sudden, Jack was no longer alone. He could see headlights in his side rearview mirror that were quickly approaching. Jack made it a point to stay in the slow lane even though the speed limit was 80 mph in this area of the state. One thing about Johnny B was that it wasn't as fast as Jack had hoped it would be when he initially made the trade with Brad. As the headlights quickly approached, Brad noticed it was from a semi-trailer truck that moved into the passing lane. Not knowing that he hadn't fully cleared Jack in the slow lane, the driver of the semi-trailer truck prematurely moved back into the slow lane and inadvertently cut Jack off. Jack quickly reacted by abruptly moving towards the right into the shallow shoulder of the road. Jack quickly lost control of the steering and veer further off to the side of the shoulder. The high center of mass of Johnny B coupled with the high speed at which it was traveling caused the RV to flip several times off to the side of the interstate. In the dark of night, the driver of the semi-trailer truck had no clue what just happened and simply continued driving on. Johnny B finally came to rest on its left side with Jack lifeless inside.

He says, "Be still and know that I am God..."

Psalm 46:10

CHAPTER 15
The Funeral

The morning was arrayed with sunlight bursting forth through the clouds and dew that blanketed the pristine grass. It was a familiar heaviness for all who were present that morning. For Hannah, it was like déjà vu. Not too long ago, the same people were gathered for her mom's funeral, but today they were gathered here for her dad's. Family, friends, current and past congregation members were once again gathered to pay their respects and give their condolences.

The ceremony took place at the committal shelter located on the south end of Miramar National Cemetery, which was only a few blocks away from the home where Hannah grew up in. She was dumbfounded as to how on earth she could lose both of her parents in so little of time.

Pastor Terry couldn't believe how not too long ago he presided over Karen's funeral, and now he was presiding over Jack's. The two ceremonies couldn't be any more similar. The stories that were shared this morning were no different than what Terry had shared just less than a month ago. He shared with the crowd some of the most humorous and embarrassing moments he and Jack shared together. He couldn't help but include Karen in those stories. Then he closed with some encouraging words and Scripture. Afterwards, Jack received full military honors for his service in the Marine Corps which comprised of a three volley firing of guns in lieu of the standard 21 gun salute followed by a live playing of taps. At the end of the service, the honor guard folded and presented Hannah with an American flag.

An urn that contained Jack's ashes sat on a small platform in the middle of the committal shelter. Jack had always expressed how he wanted to be cremated for a couple of reasons. For one, it would be less expensive for whomever was left behind to burry him; and secondly, he believed that when the Lord returned he wanted the resurrection of his earthly remains to be visually more dramatic with millions of ashes synchronously coming together rather than just one decomposed body.

After the ceremony, Hannah sat there completely numb, confused, and in disbelief. She still could not process how in a very short period of time she had lost both of her parents. She didn't know what to do. She didn't know what to think. It was then that she remembered how her dad would always remind her about how there are some things in life that we can do absolutely nothing about, situations we will find ourselves in that are beyond our control. There were a lot of sermons her dad had preached in his lifetime, but today one came particularly to mind. It was from the Book of Psalm 46:10 which read, "Be still, and know that I am God." The psalmist of this verse penned those words on behalf of God Himself who says to us, "Be still." The Hebrew word *raphah*, which the psalmist used for the words "be still" literally means to let go or to let drop. It is better translated as "cause yourself to let go" or "to take your hands off"; it also means "to relax." There will be things and challenges in our lives that we will face that are beyond our control, and God wants for us to let them go and know that He is God. God wants for us to let go of those things and allow Him to take control and work them out for our good. In the process, God affords us an opportunity to get to know Him. He allows us the opportunity to know His power, His strength, His comfort, His joy, His forgiveness, His mercy, His patience, His provision, and His healing. And the list of what God is capable of doing goes on and on. God is far more capable of doing these things better than we could. God wants for us to let go of the things that are beyond our control. Even some of the things we do have control over, God wants for us to let them go. He wants for us to drop them into His hands. The thing we need to realize is that though these situations and predicaments may be beyond our control, they are not beyond God's control. Oftentimes God wants us to make the choice to let go of things that are in our hands that we control and place them into His hands and under His control. When we put things in God's hands, it's amazing the things He is capable of doing with them. When we let go of the things that are beyond our control and trust them to God, He will work those things out in a way that will not only reveal how incredibly wonderful He is but also how much He loves and cares for us.[15]

Hannah remembered a poem from an unknown author entitled "It Depends on Whose

Hands It's In," that her dad modified and shared in that sermon. It goes something like this:

> *A basketball in my hands is an embarrassment waiting to happen, but a basketball in Michael Jordan's hands is six NBA titles*
> *It depends on whose hands it's in...*
>
> *A baseball bat in my hands is a possible infield fly homerun but surely a single to first base, but a baseball bat in Barry Bond's hands is 762 career homeruns*
> *It depends on whose hands it's in...*
>
> *A golf club is my hands results in a consistent double-bogie score card, but a golf club in Tiger Wood's hands is 14 professional major golf championships*
> *It depends on whose hands it's in...*
>
> *A rod in my hands will keep away a wild animal, but a rod in Moses' hands will part a mighty sea.*
> *It depends on whose hands it's in....*
>
> *A sling shot in my hands is an accident waiting to happen, but a slingshot in David's hands is a mighty weapon that brings down a giant.*
> *It depends on whose hands it's in...*

Two fish and five loaves in my hands are a couple of tuna sandwiches, but two fish and five loaves in Jesus' hands will feed thousands.
It depends on whose hands they're in...

Nails in my hands might produce a fairly decent wooden craft, but nails in Christ Jesus' hands will produce salvation for all of humanity.
It depends on whose hands they're in ...

As you see now it depends on whose hands it's in...

So put your concerns, your worries, your fears, your hopes, your dreams, your families and your relationships in God's Hands because...
It depends on whose hands they're in.

Hannah knew at that moment, God was holding both of her parents safely in His hands.

Family and friends approached Hannah, one after the other, hugging her and sharing their condolences. Hannah sat with tears streaming down her face as she tightly held the American flag that was presented to her. She didn't know what to make of all of this.

Hannah's husband leaned over and whispered, "Take your time baby," as he took their son Jimmy by the hand and walked over towards where some of the headstones of other veterans were laid to rest as if to give her some space.

Jimmy ran up to Hannah, looked up at his mom and said, "It'll be alright mama. Like you told me, Grandpa is with Nana now, and he's happy. So you should be happy for him."

"You're absolutely right Jimmy," replied Hannah. "Thank you for reminding mama." At that moment, Hannah's husband came up to take her by the hand as they walked to their car.

As they drove towards the exit of the cemetery, Hannah noticed a statue that was erected near the entrance. She hadn't noticed it earlier when they drove in. It was a statue of a soldier stepping out of his imprisonment. Immediately beneath the statue was the word "LIBERATION" etched into the stone base. It apparently was a memorial in honor of prisoners of war.

"Stop," Hannah told her husband.

As their car came to an abrupt halt, Hannah took the time to read the inscription that was on the plaque attached to the stone base of the statue. It read:

This statue conveys the excitement, trepidation, exhilaration and emotion of the LIBERATION moment, as the emaciated soldier steps out of the darkness into the "Sunshine of Freedom."

He portrays the hundreds of thousands who were bound in captivity by the infamy of foreign enemies.

This is to stand as an eternal legacy for our community by reminding visitors of the sacrifice of veterans during America's efforts to keep alive the hopes and dreams of freedom for the oppressed around the world.

It was at that very moment Hannah realized that the memorial statue was a symbolic reminder of her father and mother. It symbolized the liberation from their temporal and earthly life and stepping into the sunshine of freedom of their eternal and heavenly one.

ENDNOTES

1. Detachment (10/27/07)
2. The Most Important Question (11/21/04)
3. God's Voice In His Word (3/29/13)
4. Darkness Into Light (4/28/13)
5. Kadesh (2/23/03)
6. Undimmed & Unabated (3/16/03)
7. Biblical Contentment (5/2/04)
8. Trusting God (2/24/13)
9. Abana & Pharpar (9/28/03)
10. In The Same Boat (10/23/05)
11. The One Thing (5/22/05)
12. Probability (12/6/15)
13. Governing The Mind (4/6/14)
14. An Eternal Perspective (10/16/11)
15. Be Still (11/7/10)

A NOTE FROM THE AUTHOR

After serving for over 20 years in ministry, I had the wonderful privilege to take my first official sabbatical for two months in the summer of 2016. Part of that sabbatical experience consisted of a road trip up Interstate 15 North from San Diego, California to Sweet Grass, Montana and into Alberta, Canada. For me personally, the road trip served as a retreat where I spent wonderful moments alone with God in prayer and reflection.

Throughout the road trip, I lived and slept out of my 2008 Honda Element. It was a longtime dream of mine. I removed the two back seats and put in a full size inflatable air mattress. My wife took the time to sew some blackout curtains with Velcro strips that I attached over the windows for privacy at night. I had the wonderful opportunity to meet and converse with a couple of friendly folks along my journey. I also had the incredible opportunity, as a foodie, to enjoy some of the most delicious foods from local restaurants and coffee houses along the way.

The trip was originally planned to be two weeks long, but after arriving in Canada just three days in, I began to desperately miss my wife. After crossing back into the U.S. from Canada, I called her and asked her if she would be able to fly out and meet me in Las Vegas. I told her I could make it there in a couple of days. I was ecstatic when she obliged. The trip served its purpose, and I was grateful for the incredible experience.

As a pastor, I've had the wonderful opportunity to encourage and inspire people with my sermons. I'm not a long-winded preacher. I like to focus on a single point in my sermons. Each chapter of this book contains one of those main points from the many sermons that I've preached. Each main point has been notated by an endnote. The endnotes page documents the title of each of these sermons as well as the date that I preached it. The title of the book is indicative of not only my road trip up Interstate 15 North but also a compilation of 15 of my favorite sermons that I've preached that point northward, heavenward, or more specifically towards Our Heavenly Father Who loves both you and me dearly. My personal prayer is that this book will encourage faith and inspire hope.

ABOUT THE AUTHOR

Bob DeSagun served in the U.S. Navy and was later commissioned as an officer in the Marine Corps. He met and fell in love with his wife Tina in college where they got married. Immediately following his military service, he became actively involved in Christian ministry. He started and currently pastors a church in San Diego, California with The Christian and Missionary Alliance where he was licensed and ordained. He also serves as an adjunct professor for Crown College and as a trustee for Simpson University. He received his PhD from Regent University's School of Business and Leadership in Organizational Leadership with a major in Ecclesial Leadership. He has written books on the small church and small-scale ministry dynamics and also serves as a small church leadership consultant. He has been a husband for over 25 years, a father for 24, and a grandfather for 10 months.

Made in the USA
San Bernardino, CA
13 April 2018